LOVE AT THE LAVENDER FARM

LOVE
at the
LAVENDER FARM

a novella

GAIL KITTLESON

WordCrafts

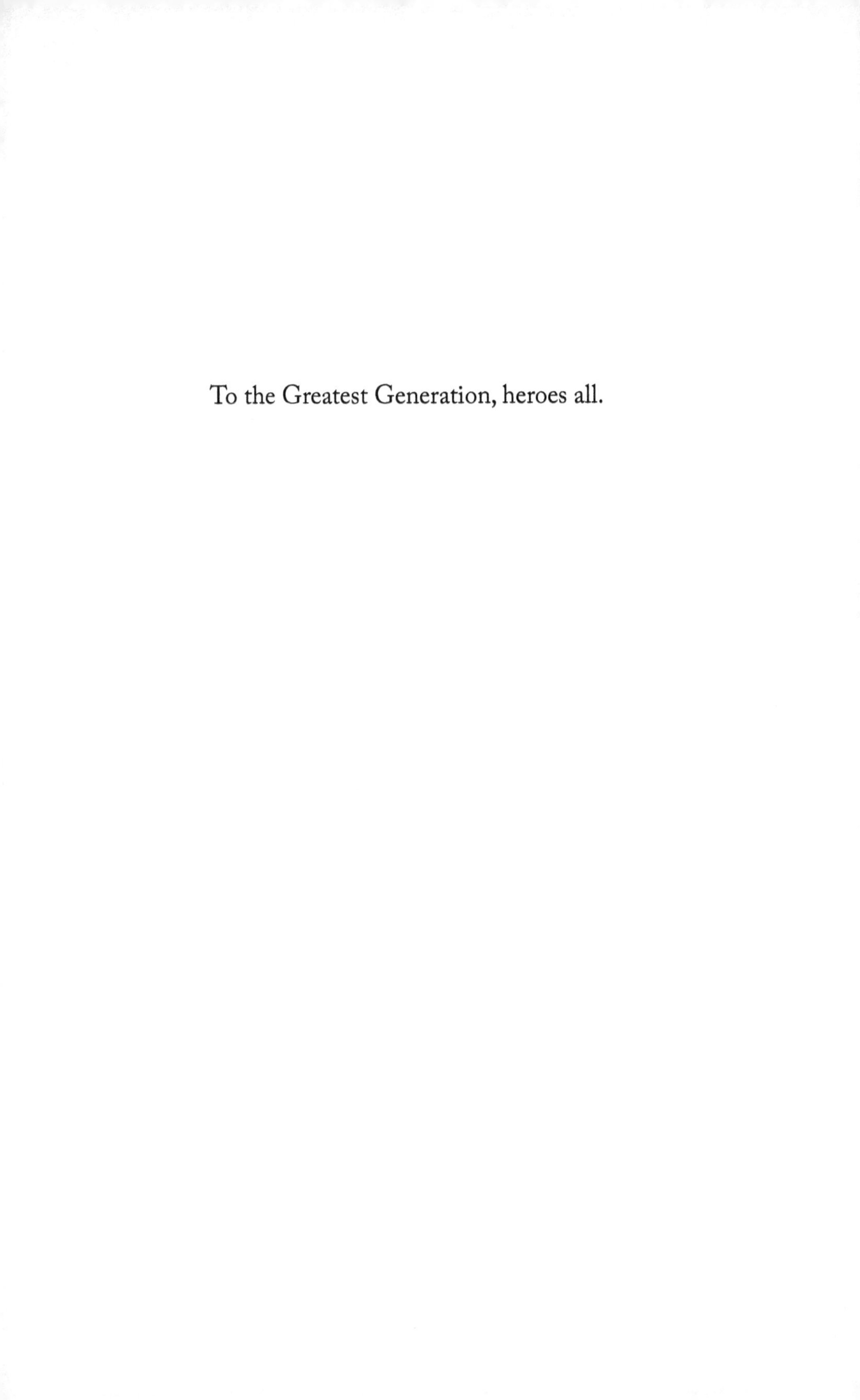

To the Greatest Generation, heroes all.

Chapter One

All morning, shade had buffered the rising heat, but as I leaned against a fencepost to read, intense Arizona sunshine penetrated my thin cotton shirt. Gabe always kept plenty of instruction books and flyers about lavender-growing in the house and shed, so I knew I would find an answer.

The most common problem with lavender occurs in the plant's root system. If the soil becomes oversaturated, clogging and displacing essential air pockets, the roots eventually drown and lose their ability to regulate the movement of water and nutrients.

They also fail to respond to sunlight and temperature and maintain internal plant pressure. Over time, a soil borne pathogen known as phytophera may permanently render the tender root hairs incapable of transporting moisture and nutrients to the plant.

"Right. So that must be what's wrong with these bushes on the edge. Too close to the ditch, and with the change in the creek's course, the ground has sunken some." A glance showed only four or five were affected—not a great concern, yet I hesitated. Gabe would be loath to part with even one lavender plant.

"But if it's this *phyto whatever*, there's nothing to do except get rid of them." I lifted my hat for a moment's relief from the heat. Air circulated against my scalp, not enough to blow ginger wisps into my face, but sufficient to cool me just a bit. These days, the slightest amount of almost anything could make a big difference.

Like a lot else around this homestead, Gabe had divined this patch of lavender. His folks emigrated from Italy to New York in the Twenties. Although he was quite young at the time, he recalled the lavender fields even today.

Once they moved to this arid country about two hours northeast of Phoenix, his vision took on new life. Even with him far away now, I could hear him extolling the beauty of those Italian fields. From the beginning of my time here, he expounded on the glories of lavender.

"Oh, the fragrance on a morning mist—heaven come to earth. Can't even describe it to you, Lyra. The scent always seemed to me like the first real breath of dawn, you know?"

I didn't know, but his powers of speech allowed me to follow his train of thought. Dawn, first breath—heaven. If he declared it so, this smell had to be good. That was all I knew, and when Gabe fell silent, his eyes said the rest. The poet in him painted pictures all day long.

In this pause, an image filled my mind like a phantom. Too soon it would be gone, so I clung to the scene—fields of lavender spreading far and wide over the Italian countryside, tinging the air with sweetness.

To grow lavender, one only must be willing to work and wait, Gabe always said. Work and wait—as usual, his meaning lasted longer than just a moment. *Working and waiting* might be the headline in the next issue of the *Arizona Republic* newspaper, for during this war, the whole of the state engaged in both.

During my youth, Papa had the willingness to work and certainly did plenty of waiting, but it did little good. Finally, he and Mama were forced to move our family to this area, fleeing a billowing cloud of dust they called the "black blizzard." That cyclone of good black topsoil from a number of states grew until it blew down on Texas without mercy.

Why Papa decided to stay in Arizona, I never knew for sure—I'd only been ten back then. But that blizzard—billowing black-grey clouds enveloping everything in sight—oh, that I remembered.

The storm left our neighbor's farmhouse in ruins, with charcoal dunes up to ten feet high inundating the yard.

A virtual parade of ramshackle trucks loaded with families' meager possessions chugged their way westward, leaving vacant homesteads behind. Some of my schoolmates had the chance to say good-bye, but others vanished overnight, swaddled in their parents' dreams of better times out West.

And then one evening, Papa announced that our turn had come.

His eyes glinted as he made the pronouncement. "We've done all we can, but the corncrib blew down today." He glanced at Mama, who had turned away. "There comes a time…"

Loaded up except for items Mama was forced to leave behind, we stopped for gasoline often. The old truck drank it like a broken-down horse guzzles water to stay alive.

Between stops, Papa attempted to console Mama—she'd been born into a better world, a finer place. There, she might have become a music teacher. But that world had vanished when she married Papa, and now, so had her piano.

Papa could never afford to fill the tank. We all watched him dicker for an ounce this way or that and hid our faces when he returned to the driver's seat, shoulders hanging and a high flush on his face.

A time or two, a weary filling station owner bartered him a couple hours of work for half a tank, and we all hung about the property like flies until he finished. Mama never moved from her seat, though, even to use the facilities.

But at one stop as we wound our way south toward Phoenix over roads not built for an old Ford like ours, a man in the gas station mentioned something of interest. That very morning, a local rancher had announced he was on the lookout for a good hired man.

Papa had asked directions to the place, and with Mama's finger tracing her jaw over and over, revved up the motor. A few miles into what looked like utter wilderness, a red-soiled scrap of a state, Papa turned at a handmade wooden sign with an arrow and passed down a lane pitted with rocks designed to rip tires apart. Fifteen minutes later, the deed was done.

The rancher, Jeb Phillips, in his fifties, shook hands with Papa, whose back straightened noticeably. Jeb helped us unload the truck, and we set up a new life. Just like that—nine of us squashed into a small cabin behind the main ranch house. But anything was better than being trapped in the truck another moment.

Jeb's wife, Minnie, welcomed us. "We've got chickens and milk and beef—I 'magine they'll be part of your husband's pay, so you oughtn't to go hungry. Besides that, these woods are full of elk and deer."

Plump and cheerful, Minnie demonstrated the secrets of cajoling water from the ancient iron pump outside the kitchen door, brought fresh linens, a pot of the best-ever chicken stew. And a hug.

Mama cried then—she wasn't one to do so, nor was I, but something about this show of kindness brought out the tears. Minnie patted Mama's arm and noted, "Looks as though you've all been through a lot. Some years back, Jeb and I…we lost our sons to the influenza."

In the nondescript kitchen, she stared off into the distance, through a window that might never have been washed. "One of 'em had a wife and three sweet little ones, but our son's wife moved back home with her parents. Can't blame her, it's true, but we've been…"

She hugged her shoulders. "At any rate, it's mighty fine to hear young voices around here again." Minnie craned her neck to study the sky rising above a mix of tall Ponderosa pine trees overlooking the rocky landscape like sentinels.

"Today things are changing—I can feel it in my bones. They can only stay bad so long, don't you think? I can feel goodness in the air. The monsoon rains stayed especially long this year. That always portends well."

Mama gave no reply, and I wasn't so sure about this "goodness in the air," but the taste of Minnie's chicken with puffy dumplings stayed with me. A good meal can make such a difference. Minnie must have seen starvation in our eyes when Papa drove into the yard, all of us dangling from the truck in every direction.

Our glances around the coarse place probably looked wary. But at least the main house and a small barn looked stable, along with a couple of out-buildings. This trip had taken its toll, yet maybe things would get better now. Maybe…what a teeming word—maybe yes, maybe no, maybe something in-between.

Still, we had all been picturing California, green and enticing, with an ocean to boot. I had let my older sisters' tales of orange and grapefruit trees heavy with fruit and a sparkling Pacific carry me away.

That night in a loft-like space we shared, my next oldest sibling, Suzie, spouted, "California, ha! This is the closest we're gonna get. We've landed smack dab in the middle of nowhere."

Trusting in Mama and Papa, I held silence. And it wasn't long before sleep befriended me—trying to rest in the rickety truck left a whole lot to be desired.

Thirteen years ago, that was, with me going on eleven. And that fall the lot of us went to school. Our clothes were shabby, for certain, but we wanted to learn.

On the first day, Gabriel Andretti made himself known, his black curly hair sparkling in the sun, his obsidian eyes a-glimmer with life. With such a small gathering of local children, all of the classes did most everything together, and Gabe drew in everybody.

No one could resist his rambunctious nature, like a pint jar of tart plum jelly, sealed with the kindliest of grins. We all marveled at him reciting Longfellow's *The Children's Hour*, the *Gettysburg Address*, *Thanatopsis*, the *Declaration of Independence*—whatever he could find to memorize—and cheered him on.

One of my brothers gave him some competition in debating, but Gabe soon outshone every on-comer in the district. He went on to win the county debate contest, and our teacher called for a party to celebrate. He was like that, the origin of fun times everyone yearned for in those days, and humble, besides.

Time passed, and one by one, all of my brothers and sisters except Suzie took off on their own. A couple of them headed back to Texas, where our oldest sister, Bea, had stayed. Before we left, she'd already been engaged to Joe, a hard-working carpenter.

Maybe the others kept in touch with her—I had no idea, but they must have heard that things had improved in the Lone Star State by now. Three more of my siblings veered westward, this stay in Arizona merely a jog in their original journey to the land of milk and honey.

The spring Suzie got married, I started working at the Andretti's fruit and vegetable stand, right on the main road a few miles from where we lived. Jeb, who had grown close to Papa since they worked together every day, went into town on Saturday mornings for supplies and offered me a ride.

From the moment I spied the fruit stand, neat and tidy, with a sizable drive leading up a hill to the family home, something altered inside. I can't explain it to this day, but the way this family had made near-desert land blossom with apple, plum, and apricot trees, a grape arbor, a large vegetable garden, and a passel of animals produced an inner shift.

The Andrettis had transformed their life in central Italy to fit here. Or coaxed this land to fit the life they left behind. By then I had entered high school and recently learned the word *ingenuity* in English class. These folks demonstrated its meaning right before my eyes.

My thinking gradually turned from vulnerability to confidence. Luca and Antonia Andretti were simply the kind of people who found a way to make things work.

Not to say that my parents weren't hard workers, but their expectations only rose so high. Once they settled in at the ranch, Papa seemed satisfied with their lot. No more dreams. As for Mama, something about leaving her piano behind seemed to steal what was left of her prospects in this life.

Suzie used to soothe me, "Mama's just tired, Lyra. Don't take it personally when she don't want to hear your lessons at night. She's plumb worn herself out with all of us."

In autumn of the year I started working at the fruit stand, Gabe graduated and went off to college. His mother had saved every penny for this venture, although Luca thought too much education frivolous. I soon learned that when Antonia Andretti got an idea in her mind, it intended to stay put.

That first summer when he came home, Gabe brought with him the idea of growing lavender. One of his horticulture classes had encouraged him in this. Of course, the Andrettis had harvested lavender in Italy, but the land here, Luca thought, would not sustain a crop.

From the time Gabe returned, he expounded upon the virtues of this plant. It was as if he'd found his passion. Lavender attracted bees from the woods, for one thing, and bee pollination increased the productivity of all manner of crops. Besides that, lavender held healing properties, helping people sleep, warding off infection, and boosting immunity to disease.

"Lavender's tough," he maintained. "Doesn't need a lot of rain, just enough to get by. There's not a big market for it here, not yet, but those fields back in the Old Country turn into pressed oil. Over there, doctors use the oil for an antiseptic. Did you know that in the Great War, lavender became the main ingredient in healing wounds?

"Guess it grew wild in some parts of Italy in the beginning, but when other crops failed, the people realized lavender could be cultivated. I know that nobody else around here has a field, but just look at the rosemary growing wild out there!"

He spread his arm toward the Mogollon Rim, a limestone and sandstone escarpment walling the canyon—Pine Canyon. Between there and the Rim, hilly land grew mostly spindly oaks, holly, and manzanita bushes, alligator pine, and the tall, stately Ponderosa Pine.

"Nothing worth its salt 'cept for lumber," Luca maintained.

But Gabe saw only possibilities. "Not much difference between rosemary and lavender, I say. Just look at the few lavender plants we already have around the yard—we never have to worry about them, do we? No! They just keep on growing."

His father knew all about those fields back in the Old Country but had little time for Gabe's idea. "Will lavender put food on the table like a good crop of corn? Will it feed the cattle like hay or sorghum? I know you remember the old days, but this is a different time, a different place. And as you say, there's no market."

Not one to argue, Gabe took in his daddy's words and pondered. Most likely, he analyzed this with his professors in the fall, but never gave up on his ambition. Like those farmers in Italy, he embraced the potential, and with no cost to Luca, he started keeping bees.

Antonia encouraged him and learned beekeeping herself. At work in the stand, I sometimes spied her out tending the hives, completely at ease, her chatter carrying on the hot summer air.

Gabe stopped by at the stand often and one day he said his mother had a way with the bees—perfect for when he had to be gone. "Some women wouldn't even think to tangle with them." His smile matched the lights in his eyes. "But Mama's a tough one. She may seem a little harsh at times, but you can't beat her good Sicilian heart."

Over the next year, Antonia worked on Luca, and the summer after his graduation, Gabe asked if I would like to help him plant a lavender field. He showed me a hill on the property that his father had agreed to let him use.

Another good thing about this crop, Gabe maintained, was that the herds of elk and mule deer around this area avoided lavender. Strange, since they devoured nearly every other green, growing item.

I had always loved working with the soil, even this recalcitrant stuff that dared you to grow something. And so it was—Gabe and I spent several days measuring, digging out rocks, raking the soil into obedience, and planting small bushes ordered from a seed catalog.

During a break, as a wisp of breeze blew in from the west and lemonade satisfied our thirst, Gabe launched his proposal. I had turned seventeen that fall and just graduated high school.

Gabe had been talking about being willing to work hard and sacrifice. "In the end, we'll have a beautiful field to show for this day's labor. And there *will* be a market, I'm sure of that." Then all of a sudden his eyes darkened, his voice lowered, and his tone set my back upright against a front porch pillar.

"We maybe won't have a lot at first, but I've got a chance at a post as a state agronomist. Wouldn't pay much, and yet…" He glanced around his parents' land. "I think we could make it, you and me.

"We'd have to live here with the folks for a while. I'm afraid Mama might be a little overbearing at first, but we'd be together. We could save up enough to buy our own place."

My throat dried out like a shriveled orange peel. Somewhere between my lips and my lungs, my breathing halted.

"You and me," Gabe repeated, peering into my soul. "Our dreams are as green as your eyes, and I think we can make it together, if you're willing."

Willing? The whole world knew I'd lost my heart to Gabe when he sent me a Valentine back in my sophomore year. I figured he'd dispersed tokens like this to several girls, but the homemade artwork, a drawing of lavender in bloom, was still stuck in my bedroom mirror.

> *"Roses are red,*
> *Lavender is sweet,*
> *You are pretty and*
> *I think you're neat!*

Through my years of gangly legs and a sea of irascible red hair that defied my efforts to tame it, Gabe always had a friendly word for me. Somewhere along the way, he took to calling me Lyralee.

In lieu of a response, he slid over and took my hand. "Would you consider marrying me, Lyra? I've loved you for years—don't know how I could live without your freckles."

Well. The details lie close to my heart, but on that day that now seems so long ago, Gabe grasped my waist and lifted me in a dizzy circle. My skirt swayed around him, and I felt as though I'd been swung between heaven and earth.

After all of this time, I still can't quite believe it at times. Never did I imagine this man wanting to spend his life with me.

He brought me down so our eyes met. "So, beautiful Lyra, my girl. Even though some of my ideas make your eyebrows dance, I'm willing to work hard. Willing to sacrifice."

I simply stared at him. Marry Gabe Andretti? Live here in this lovely place? I was so moonstruck I forgot his warning about his mother's temperament—forgot, too, that Mama had an aversion to us marrying Catholics.

Nothing mattered except the message in Gabe's eyes. He had faith in me, faith in the future. He was willing to work, willing to sacrifice. At some point, my tongue must have recalled its powers, because here I was, some years later, tending the lavender field we planted that day.

Chapter Two

A cry rose from the side yard, where our daughter Bella had been helping Grandma Antonia watch her baby brother, Luca, named for Gabe's daddy. At three, Bella had become Grandma and Mommy's big helper.

Last November, Gabe said good-bye to his father exactly a week before little Luca entered our lives. To have Grandpa taken so quickly after developing pneumonia stunned us. Not one to call a doctor, Luca worsened overnight and by the time Gabe brought Doctor Lawson out to the farm, little could be done to save him.

So much sadness and so much joy packed into a few days. A newborn son to hold close, but his grandfather taken from this world before his time. Antonia exclaimed over both.

"How can-a this be? My Luca gone from the world so fast, yet this baby boy in my arms?"

And then on December seventh, the day that will live in infamy, our world turned upside down. We were listening to the New York Philharmonic orchestra that Sunday afternoon on the radio, as usual.

The year 1941 was coming to a close with farm prices holding steady. We sold milk and cream to the local store for a good profit and grew enough vegetables to keep us healthy. I'd spent most of the fall canning tomatoes, corn, string beans, and meat with Antonia supervising.

She had taught me to make cheese from goats' milk, too. Besides that, Gabe had showed me how to milk our cow and the herd of seven goats. "The perfect number, Lyralee, like the hills around Rome."

Over the year, the fruit stand brought in steady cash. Antonia's lavender soap and lavender-infused honey were nowhere else to be found in these parts, and a few local women with extra money in the household frequented our supply.

And we offered something else. Where but here could courting young men find nosegays to pin on their sweethearts' sleeves for important events?

As Gabe saw it, we could soon add lavender oil to our inventory. To that end, he sent for the delicate glass tubing required to fashion a distiller and had already captured a few small bottles of oil.

We'd butchered a hog and a beef a couple of weeks back. Smoked hams lined the rafters in our dug-out pantry, along with sausage, dried beef and jerky. For Christmas, we'd feasted on a goose and the trimmings and looked forward to a similar 1942.

Everyone pitched in all week long and welcomed this Sunday afternoon respite. Then an announcement interrupted the ethereal music issuing from the program. I had just been hoping Mama was listening when alarm passed through our parlor like electricity. Our President described a Japanese attack on our Navy in a place we'd never heard of but would never forget.

Pearl Harbor…Pearl Harbor. Such a lovely-sounding name for such a dastardly deed!

We huddled together, Gabe holding Bella and a sleeping Luca in his arms as Mrs. Roosevelt took the microphone. Something about her calling attention to the sacrifices we would all need to make made my eyes smart.

Antonia, momentarily shushed by the news, paced between the kitchen and living room. Her heavy steps reverberated, as though she might pound away her anxiety.

War had already encompassed most of Europe, and the Italian dictator Mussolini had joined Herr Hitler's Third Reich. Nazis most likely deployed relatives of the Andretti family still living in Italy.

In France, where my grandparents—my mother's ancestors—had lived until adulthood, everything had fallen apart. Surely my parents were aghast right now. When the Nazi army invaded, how could it be that the French put up such a paltry fight?

Now we experienced our own national shock. From the moment of the announcement, every honest American man thought of leaving home and hearth to join the fight. Including Gabe, of course. As the sole male provider on a family farm, he might have waited, but not Gabe—he always took the initiative.

Wait? We both knew he wouldn't wait. Always wanting to do his part, he had joined the National Guard before graduating from high school.

On that fated afternoon, December 7, 1941, even as he clutched our babies closer, his expression said good-bye. He would be leaving, no doubt about it.

But in February, the government issued an Executive Order. Exclusion Order number 9066 classified Americans of Japanese and Italian descent as enemy aliens. That meant if you were born in Italy, as Gabe was, even though you were a naturalized citizen, you might be seen as a threat.

When the news reached Antonia, she let loose. "They think-a we are the Mafia? They think-a we love Mussolini?" She banged her fist on the table and Luca began to cry.

Gabe led her outdoors, where their voices carried through the screen door. "This is-a why we came here from the East. I wouldn't let-a those boys call you a *wop* or a *dago* or a *guinea*. You know, some of those so-called brilliant ones even think our people are a separate race?"

"Mama, I don't care what they think. I'm an American, and they can't keep me from serving. I will find a way, and I'm not alone. I bet more Italian-Americans are signing up than any other nationality."

"But your Papa's brother in Philadelphia… They confiscated his short-wave radio!"

"Mama, Mama. Calm down. This is Arizona, remember? You

and Papa did the right thing, moving here—nobody's coming out to our place to confiscate anything. I'll go down this week and speak with the draft board if I need to."

So he did. And just as he won his debates, Gabe secured an Army-green uniform and orders to report for active duty in one week. Not to mention what he lost—such a gorgeous head of black curly hair.

Although Antonia could not have been prouder that day, at the same time, the reality of Gabe going to war set her off. Would the commanders treat him like everyone else? Would he be ostracized?

This drove Gabe to distraction. "Mama, stop! They want men to fight, don't you realize that? If they treat anyone unfairly, it's the Negro men who are trying to sign up. Doesn't make one bit of sense, but the Army's keeping them from bearing arms."

Ah… Antonia's anger quieted, but not for long. I began to dread times when no one would be here to mollify her fiery spirit. But she always did more than her share, especially with our two little ones. Since Gabe's unit left for training at Fort Sill with the Army's Forty-fifth Division, she has become our mainstay.

Always a supporter of Gabe, even if her husband might have been slow to latch onto some of his ideas, she wrote to him twice a week and sent him packages. This activity became a big production for Bella, who included hand-drawn pictures for Daddy.

Antonia went so far as to purchase a brownie camera to keep Gabe informed on the state of the crops and the children's growth. In every packet, she also included a stash of lavender, since he loves it so.

When she read a letter from him aloud, she blanched at certain phrases such as *basic combat training*. The words came forth, but like spittle, clipped and shunted.

Combat, we would all like to deny.

By the day, the worry lines in her forehead deepened, but not once did she break down. Her child, her last born—learning the art of war. This defied everything that motivated her people to leave the Old Country.

"We fought the war to end them all, and now this! *Santo cielo!*"

Good heavens—how often Mama said that in English as we were growing up. So often, she followed this exclamation with, "What next?"

Our small parish lay less than a half-mile away, and whenever Antonia disappeared, I knew where to find her. In the sanctuary, women lighted candles daily for their husbands and sons. Surely now, she must have been thinking of Leonardo, too, one of her twins, a priest in Mexico. The rest of her children, all girls, had scattered and were rearing their own families.

For the first time, our household had subscribed to a daily newspaper, read mostly by Antonia, grim-faced, in lantern or fire light after the children were in bed each evening. Something about this evening ritual heartened her.

"Thirty-six divisions in the Army now. One million, four hundred thousand men, when six months ago, there were only six-hundred and thirty." She found a short article about Joe DiMaggio's parents being banned from the bay where Mr. DiMaggio made his living by fishing.

"What-a they think? He's a gonna bring Nazis here after all these years?"

Facts like these swirled the parlor like ghosts, either from the newspaper or from the weekly letter Gabe sent to Antonia. Some arrived for me, too, but so far she had not asked about the contents.

"In August, Gabriel will go to Louisiana to fight a pretend war. Our neighbor passed through there once when he was young and following the work. Worthless land, he said… infested by swamps."

My half-listening failed to deter her from repeating details out loud. While she studied the paper and proclaimed her findings, I sewed clothes for Bella and Luca. Grandma's old foot-pedal machine, the one thing I took when I left home, was getting quite the work-out.

In December after the maneuvers, Gabe hurried home on a short leave. Privately he told me about a commander named Patton, a real character. But downstairs, he was careful about what he said and instructed us, "Don't tell anyone what you know. Loose lips sink ships, so keep mum about anything I tell you."

Bella pranced the room, trying out this new rhyme. "Ships… lips."

Antonia exploded when he disclosed his unit's sketchy plans for the new year. In a few months, they would sail directly to North Africa, to invade Sicily.

"Sicily!" Antonia became animated. "Your grandmother's father—my grandfather—came to Italy from there back in 1880. Who knows, you might see the city of his birth."

During these evenings, great rustlings began in the attic, trunks and boxes being dragged here and there. Gabe explained, "She's searching for papers documenting our ancestors, whatever good that will do. For one thing, they'll all be written in Italian."

What she came up with intrigued us. One of her grandfather's brothers emigrated at about the same time as Luca and Antonia, but settled in Middletown, Connecticut. Who knew how far and wide the family had spread?

When Gabe heard this, he noted, "Just like the honeybees the early settlers brought from Europe. There was no honey in America before that. Some bees escaped their hives, though, and started their own colonies in the woods."

"I remember you believed that if we planted lavender, the blossoms would draw the bees from the forest, and this has proved true." Antonia beamed at Gabe's wisdom, and allowed that had Luca lived longer, he would have changed his mind.

Her evening searches proved perfect for Gabe and me—an idyllic time, each of us determined to make this a happy period. Hours with the children, long walks in the moonlight, each action a reinstatement of our mutual commitment.

"You know," he whispered on his last night. "You are so strong, my Lyralee. I never have to worry how things are going back here—always know you're keeping the children safe. And though you may not realize it, you have a quieting effect on Mama."

"You think so? I'm not so sure about that, but I know you're doing what you have to. I'm proud of you, too."

Then he left again—we all watched him board the train. Antonia fought me on this, but I insisted, so that Bella and Luca might form their own memories. In the next years, how often would I remind them, "Remember when Daddy hugged you and waved to us from the train steps?"

Ah yes, they made memories of him standing in the doorway of this noisy monster, also their first sight of a train. Each evening after they fell asleep, Antonia pulled out her satchel of letters. Of course, Gabe could not disclose details of his journey across the Atlantic, but she had dredged up a cousin out on the East Coast.

She re-established contact with him, and he promised to keep an eye on departures and report his findings. At this, Antonia did a little victory dance, but when she wrote to Gabe, he argued.

"Mama, out here I'm a single worker bee in a huge hive. Your cousin won't have any idea of our whereabouts."

"Ah, maybe so. But he knows your unit number." For Antonia, this settled the question. An Italian cousin held immense power.

Late in May, a telegram arrived. I had never seen one before, but it took only seconds to decipher. "Lyra, meet me in Albuquerque May twenty-sixth. Two-day pass, one day together."

Albuquerque? He might have asked me to fly to Saturn, but Antonia had plenty of Italian cards in her pocket.

"Albuquerque? Ah. I know someone who drives a truck up there once a week. Let me see. Maybe you can ride with him."

And so it was. Twenty-four hours together before Gabe left the States, and true to his word, this fellow whom Antonia trusted, a man in his sixties doing what he could for the war effort, got me there and back.

When I thanked him, he shrugged. "My two grandsons are goin' over there. I know how it is."

People always use *whirlwind* to describe chaotic events crammed together into a small time or space. They're right. A whirlwind evening, morning, and afternoon with Gabe passed like quicksilver. Then I wiped away more tears as I stood waving at the train station.

Three days away from Bella and Luca. I came home longing for them, but with priceless memories—Gabe's scent, his voice, his tenderness. Enough to see me through. He told me about the men he would be with, the Thunderbirds. Many of them were native Indians from Oklahoma, New Mexico, Colorado, and Arizona.

"They've taught me more than I learned in our formal training. They're born warriors, with fighting in their blood, and we'll all watch out for each other."

Back home, I avoided mentioning the fighting part. With things back to normal, I also forgot all about that Italian cousin of Antonia's, but several days after I returned, she received a letter from him with the sort of specifics she craved.

"My sources say the Forty-fifth Infantry will leave Hampton Roads Port of Embarkation early in June. Attack transports, cargo ships, oilers, ten destroyers and a cruise ship—I believe the Philadelphia—are being readied. What a vast Armada… our boy will not be alone."

Suddenly "your boy" had become "our boy."

On June 4, Gabe's first V-mail from aboard ship arrived.

> *Nothing but the Atlantic as far as the eye can see. You can imagine what a tight squeeze it is in here—well, maybe not.*
>
> *The sea air can be invigorating, but I have to hold my breath down below. Going up on deck reminds me of why we're doing this… For freedom.*
>
> *I've made a friend down in the kitchen. He's from Georgia and signed up to fight. His muscles are twice the size of mine, yet so far they've only let him work in the kitchen because he's Negro. I guess that's true with some Italian-Americans too, but somehow I managed to pass muster.*

Kisses to Bella and Luca. Can't think about how they must be growing, or I get too sad. Hate to miss it all.

I'll be home as soon as possible. It helps to know you've got everything under control.

Always yours,

Gabe

After that, word became scarce. Unfortunately Antonia had no cousin living in North Africa, where Gabe's ship was scheduled to land. Members of the family remaining in Sicily surely had evacuated or hunkered down, fearing for their lives.

Like most other American families, we were forced to rely on the nightly newscasts for information. Italian cousins couldn't be everywhere.

When little was forthcoming, Antonia, undeterred, pulled out Gabe's letters, and that cousin's. With phrases and gestures, she re-created the image of Gabe for the children.

"Your Papa travels in safety. This we know for certain. Just think, all of those other ships just to protect your papa."

I retreated into silence. What good would voicing my fears do? Such a huge ocean and so many German torpedo boats—the evening news always found a way to add an element of terror.

On July tenth, our newscaster detailed the invasion of Sicily—British, American, and Canadian troops landing between Licata and Siracusa, Sicily under General Eisenhower's command. He emphasized that this was the largest amphibious invasion in history.

Every night we listened and pondered. Antonia somehow found a map so we could follow the cities conquered by our troops. Each day seemed an eternity, dreading the evening news, yet hungering for details.

Finally, we had harvested the lavender. Its lovely essence satiated the air here on the farm as summer deepened.

On July twenty-second, the news thrilled us.

Civilians cheered the soldiers of Patton's Seventh Army as they rolled into Palermo, Sicily, the largest enemy city captured up to this time. U.S. troops of General Geoffrey Keyes' "Provisional Corps," part of George S. Patton's Seventh Army claimed the victory.

Now for the arrest and demise of the Italian Dictator, Mussolini.

And then onward to Italy—roll on, troops, roll on!

On July twenty-fifth, Antonia gave way to shouts, "Mussolini has been arrested—the fascists have fallen! Now the good people of Italy will rise up against that German demon Hitler."

I hoped she was right. But would Italian peasants demoralized by the Nazi presence have the wherewithal to stand against their oppressors? Clearly, Antonia believed this to be true.

August arrived, 1943, and with it word that the Battle for Sicily had ended. Bella, seeing my tears gush, screwed up her face.

"Mama cry!"

"Yes, honey. But it's for joy." That night, we listened to the radio even more closely and basked in this victory.

Bravo for our boys in the Mediterranean! Beginning with their landing in southeastern Sicily, in just thirty-nine days, our boys have won the victory!

Operation Husky has completed its goal. The besieged island of Sicily has been liberated.

Beyond this, more good will come. We can all look forward to the invasion of Italy, leading us to the Nazi stronghold in France and finally into the heart of Berlin, itself.

September brought the signing of an armistice with the Allies. Surely now, our troops would quickly defeat the Germans occupying Italy. To Bella's applause, Antonia cried, "Perhaps by Christmas, your Papa will come home."

When I tucked her into bed, Bella murmured, "Daddy come home."

"Yes, we must pray he comes home. But we do not know when."

Chapter Three

Soil for lavender farming should be well-drained and not too rich. Sandy soil works well, but lavender may not survive in clay. It pays to amend dense or poorly drained soil with large amounts of mulch, gravel, sand, or compost.

Here I was, returning to Gabe's favorite instruction booklet for advice. We already had rocky, poor soil, so caring for our lavender plants mostly required patience. Sometimes I wished there were more I could do, but during autumn and winter, we mainly watched and waited.

That morning, though, I needed action. Shoveling and hauling buckets full of pebbles and sand from the creek filled the first hour—making the soil even more rocky couldn't hurt, right? Working in the mixture up and down the rows kept me occupied till noon, when my blouse was soaked and my feet ached.

At times, Antonia got on my nerves. Nearly everything that exasperated her about the war was something no one had power to change. Forever angry about the evacuation and unfair treatment of Italian-Americans on the West Coast, she still launched questions at the government almost every day.

"How you think-a our sons can fight but we're-a not patriotic? Why don't you-a ask a *mother* if her son's blood is good enough?" Sometimes I would see her out doing chores, raising her fist between the goat pen and the lavender field, still shouting at the President.

"How come-a you tell the FBI they can arrest our people, Mister

Presidente? Same-a day our Italian sons went down to register to fight—day after Pearl Harbor! They fight for our country—*this-a* country!"

Her informants, who lived in various parts of the States, kept her in stories and statistics. Probably they were family members of her friends at church, as upset as she was and eager to feed this never-ending fire more fuel.

Even 1942's federal removal of Italians from enemy-alien status on Columbus Day did little to mollify the situation. Hearing President Roosevelt on the radio saying that Italians were once more considered patriotic citizens ought to have helped, but in some quarters, only stirred things up more.

So did word that Gabe had been right about the number of Italians signing up to fight. More of them than any other nationality were deployed, according to some expert Antonia knew.

But that day, as I came in, weary and hungry, she temporarily forgot her private war with the government and seized the moment to shine, ladling her steaming minestrone into a bowl for me. This was the Antonia I knew at the beginning, more caring than irate.

Then she set Bella to rubbing my feet.

"*Povera Mamma*! Poor Mama's toes!"

Our little girl made everything into a tune those days, and my feet were no exception. After a twenty-minute pampering, I pushed back my chair, ready to go out again.

"We might try planting some spike lavender next season—it would be good for our soaps. What do you think?"

"These winters get too cold for it. Maybe we should try lavandin."

Hmm. Dutch lavender. A hybrid of English and spike lavender, not the highest quality of oil, but oh, the blossoms!

"It would be fun to surprise Gabe with a new variety, wouldn't it? I'll start hoeing up a patch."

"No." Antonia changed in a flash. I had seen this look in her eyes before. Not to be ignored, she pulled me to the window. "Look out there. You have done so much already, and the field looks fine.

The rows will still be there tomorrow. You should be taking a rest every afternoon."

A nap did sound good. But then, meaningfully, Antonia patted her stomach.

Tears flooded my eyes as she stood there, immovable and right as usual. I had known I was expecting again—known and not known. But with Gabe gone, so much to do, and all of our worries, how could I possibly be?

Antonia patted her stomach again. Touched her hips with the sides of her hands as if to say, *Well, are you going to acknowledge the truth or not?*

Something about her indignant stance and the way Bella started teasing little Luca in the background ignited a fury in me. In the heat outside the window, a misled bird chirped as if dawn were just breaking.

No one likes to be told what to do… or how to do it. Most of the time, I hadn't minded, but on that day, I did. Antonia's eyes snapped as I hurried outside.

She might reign here—that was her right. She and Gabe's father built this place from nothing. But now that Gabe had left, I had to rediscover my niche—after all, I belonged here, too.

Everywhere on our land holly bushes sprang forth, sometimes getting out of hand and growing into small trees. Behind the milk house, such an unwanted plant had taken over, but today its luck ran out.

Out of sight from the house, all alone, I leaned against the small building to open the door. Then I reached inside for Gabe's axe, hauled it to the holly bush, and plunged it into the thick of a low branch.

Whack!

Halfway through. It wouldn't take much more to start a brush pile.

Another blow.

Craack!

The sound strengthened me.

Three branches later, huffing like a cow on ice, something bade me stop. About a rod away hovered Antonia, holding Luca in one arm with Bella's hand in hers.

From behind, the sun formed auras around their heads. Two generations, with me smack in the middle of them. A swift recollection overtook me—a new neighbor moved in down the road recently, and yesterday we had met him.

Full of information, for the government sent him to supervise war work in a Phoenix airplane manufacturing plant, he held us spellbound. Before the time ended, he told us his wife, four children, and father-in-law, Bernardo, would be living here with relatives for the duration of the war.

For safety, he would rather not have them in Phoenix, he said. As he spoke, a bomber flew overhead, and he glanced up. "The skies are going to be full of them, with so many pilots training here."

The meeting planted hope in all of us—new people to get to know, a family added to our community. In this respect, I had a lot in common with Antonia—nothing I liked better than meeting strangers.

Antonia's minestrone had already found its way to their home. Their last name—Bartiromo—made this a given. I made my own quiet plans to welcome the wife, a Spanish speaking woman with children all around her, perhaps with a basket of lavender soap and some tea.

But at that moment, as I paused with Gabe's axe in hand, our new neighbor's closing statements caught me by the throat.

"So much work to be done. Arizona's flooded with airfields and soldiers, and the Army's moving a whole division from Fort Polk to Camp Laguna, a huge training camp out in the Sonoran Desert.

"I've met the transportation officer—talk about having your work cut out for you." He shielded his eyes from the sun for a moment before turning them on me.

"But you're doing the toughest work of all—waiting for your husband. Thank you for sending him over there to fight for us."

"He wouldn't have it any other way." It was easy to cast the light on Gabe, but this fellow's message touched me. *Waiting will be the toughest work....* I thought about the child I carried—such a gift! Yet this little one's arrival also required me to wait.

I would not change my condition, oh no! What better way to welcome Gabe home than with another child to hear his bedtime stories? Now there will be three sets of footsteps, three sets of welcoming arms, unique young personalities in our world.

This thought quieted my spirit as I put the axe away.

Bella ran to me, big-eyed. "Mama, you are so strong!"

Yes, my child. Yes I am, and I am claiming my place here. It's just the waiting that gets to me.

Antonia still poised a distance away with Luca, studying me. I imagined her puzzling that another woman could be so different, that my opinions often collided with hers.

But here we were, the two of us. We'd gotten along pretty well thus far, and I vowed to watch my attitude from now on.

Because my mother-in-law was so verbose, I sometimes had difficulty separating my thoughts from hers. A day without an outburst from her had become rare, and even when she rocked Luca and sang to him, she interrupted herself.

Perhaps she thought of rocking Gabriel twenty-some years ago. Perhaps she visualized him in dreadful fighting right now. In the firelight on one September evening, her skin glowed, and a younger Antonia made herself known. Skin of burnt gold, a striking Italian beauty.

Once, she had been the one expecting. First, she produced twins, a boy and a girl, and then a succession of three girls before Gabriel. She and Luca lived a rough life, making do with nearly nothing during the darkest days of the thirties, to owning land

and feeding themselves, to even making a little cash from the fruit stand.

When I first met her, her biggest worry was for Gabriel's brother. "Just two boys in the family, and one a priest." Antonia's pride seeped through each word. But in '37, Gabe's brother Lorenzo accepted a call to work with the poor in Mexico.

With two sons away now, she stared down the road, awaiting the postman each morning. And each day hollowed out her frown. Then one day, a letter arrived from Lorenzo. She stopped on the way from the mailbox to open it and entered the house with excitement all over her face.

Waving several small sheets of paper, she hollered, "It's from Lorenzo! *Sono così grato!*" She plopped in the armchair and read aloud, half in English, half in Italian.

"His brothers in Italy are sheltering refugee children whose parents have been killed." She lowered her voice.

"These little ones are mostly Jews…children who have no homes now, nothing at all. Sometimes the monks make trips up into mountain villages with them, to save their lives." Watching Bella out playing beside the lavender field, she shook her head.

"He cannot write so often, but somehow, made sure this letter came to us. He asked us to send help—he will make sure what we send gets to these children. He says we will be hidden angels of mercy."

She folded her hands and sat for a while in silence. "We will do what we can."

"Absolutely." A thrill ran the length of my spine. Something we could do to make this woeful world a bit brighter—a way to make a difference.

And so we did our best—Antonia perhaps better than her best. She shared the letter with our local priest, leading to other families getting involved.

All the while I helped, mostly by sewing clothes to include in the packets. The patterns, just like the dresses and pants I made for Bella and Luca, ran through my mind at night during wakeful hours. *If I cut a bit less right here and double stitch over on this side, I can make one more outfit from the same amount of cloth.*

When a letter finally arrived from Gabe, Antonia read it aloud, as always. Yet I noticed she was able to set it aside as she gathered items for another package.

Through Lorenzo, she had found the precise balm for her soul—a mission to carry out. I breathed deeper, watching her pour herself into this project.

Since my attack on the holly bush, calmness had overtaken me. Could I explain this? No, but the transformation brought welcome quietude. And during those weeks after Lorenzo's letter, an irrevocable truth rose in my consciousness.

No one in our family ever talked about the last war—Papa refused to, like most former soldiers. But during his early adulthood another great change had occurred. After the war, his family emigrated from France to the States.

They had lost their home to the fighting, and their livelihood. During that time, his father made a significant decision to change the family name from Steinberg to Stanton—yes, they were Jewish. Having learned this from an aunt during my high school years, I still marvel that Papa never brought himself to pass on to us this vital part of our history.

Gabriel knew about this, but not Antonia. And until then as I considered those refugee children suffering simply for being born Jewish, I had barely acknowledged the truth myself.

Yet as surely as the sun rose each morning, Jewish blood flowed through my veins. The thought haunted me. If we lived in Europe right now, our Bella and Luca might have been among those children who had to be send away, or whose parents the Nazis killed. They would be refugees, too. Oh, the courage and love of those who sent their children away to save their lives, knowing they would never again see them!

Learning that our government refused to raise the quota on

Jewish immigrants made me ill. What ailed the powers in Washington? Would it help to write President Roosevelt?

I remembered reading about the *Kindertransport,* with British organizations working together to bring Jewish children from Nazi Germany, Czechoslovakia, and Poland to England. At that time, Italian Jews were out of reach, with Mussolini in power.

But now, this terrible scourge had spread throughout Europe, even through France—who was helping the children there? In Italy, Antonia said, Lorenzo's brothers were doing as much as they could. I had to believe the same to be true in France.

More than ever, Gabe's willingness to fight against the evil Reich made me proud. But the fight was going so slowly—I could understand Antonia's impatience.

Here it was, the end of 1943, and the Allies had advanced only seventy miles beyond Salerno since September—in four months of fighting. They gained the most ground during September, but progress had slowed and so many American soldiers had died, a newspaper article recently compared this situation with the bungling tardiness of Allied efforts in World War I.

Gabe's letters had stopped, so I assumed his unit prepared to invade somewhere else on Italy's coast. The reports gave no comfort at all—such a precarious time, with two previous invasions resulting in great loss of life and no progress.

When they retreated, the Germans raided farms and destroyed what was left of crops. Across Italy, citizens had begun to starve.

"*Dio Mio*! These are our people."

When Antonia felt most desperate, she threw her rosary over the clothesline. With Bella in school, I spent more time with Luca. After we walked her to school, we worked outdoors. So much needed to be done with the lavender, once it was all cut. Luca and I retreated to a cool, dark shed where the lavender stalks had been hung in bunches to dry. Gabe built this shed specifically for the drying, with slats high in the walls to promote circulation, but also with protection from moisture. No fungus or mold allowed here.

Since the monsoons were sparse this year, by late September, the bundles had nearly dried, so I began debudding the stems, a simple process, yet never monotonous. I held the buds over a large tray and rolled them between my hands.

This took time, but the scent reminded me of Gabe, and gradually, I filled several bowls. Luca loved this secluded place, and Sam, our gentle collie, stood watch right outside the door. So many trips back and forth for Luca, pretending to feed Sam the stalks.

When we finished the debudding, Luca helped me spread the stalks around the outside of our house to ward off mice and scorpions. By the time we ate our midday meal, we both were ready for naps.

After a morning completing these simple but necessary tasks, I fell asleep upstairs with a lighter heart. Gabe and the lavender wound together, inseparable.

Weeks passed, bringing an early snowfall that delighted Bella and made Luca's eyes sparkle. Nothing like smushing this wonderful cold, wet stuff in your hands for the first time.

One evening just before Christmas, Bella asked if Daddy would be coming home. Antonia was about to say something, but I took over.

"Not this year, honey. Maybe next Christmas. But Grandma sent him your pictures for gifts, so he will be thinking of you."

Chapter Four

O n January twenty-second, we wakened to this:

The Italian Campaign continues today as some fifty thousand Allied troops stage an amphibious landing at Anzio, 33 miles south of Rome.

Codenamed Operation Shingle, this effort to bypass the strong German defenses along the Gustav Line bodes well. The Fifth Army was checked temporarily only 20 miles (32 km) north of Naples, on the Volturno River and more permanently on the Garigliano River, while the Eighth Army, surging from Calabria up the Adriatic coast, has been held by the enemy on the Sangro River.

Autumn and midwinter have passed without the Allies making any notable impression on the one-hundred-mile Gustav Line. This runs for 100 miles from the mouth of the Garigliano through Cassino and over the Apennines to the mouth of the Sangro.

Surely, this landing will change everything. With such a short distance to the capitol city, this new entrance at Anzio will advance our cause without delay.

If only news reporters possessed the gift of prophecy. Unfortunately, just the opposite of their predictions happened—our troops at Anzio also became bogged down under a merciless German defense.

Despite her package-sending project, the clouds in Antonia's eyes grew into thunderheads. The clothesline housed her rosary on a near-permanent basis.

But one day, in the midst of horrific reports of Luftwaffe bomb-ings and the Allies being unable to break out from the fighting at Anzio, a newspaper carried a heartfelt story. In the midst of death and destruction, the Red Cross catered a wedding there between an American nurse and a soldier.

Antonia cried, "Ah, Lyra—love conquers all. Even this war."

Do you really think so? This was what I wanted to ask, but I kept it to myself.

In spite of grim news from the battlefield, this story gave Antonia some light. She began working on her project every day with a group from the church, and I relished being here alone with Luca.

With just us two, the passage of hours seemed simpler, more natural somehow. My fingers grew numb from hours of sewing, but the clothing for Antonia's mission increased little-by-little, and our new little one would not lack for nappies and sleeping togs.

One morning a letter arrived from my long-lost older sister Suzie. Suzie, who never did anything to displease our parents and was always quick to point out when I did. Seeing her handwriting on the envelope, I got a bit queasy.

Since we parted on less than the best terms, I hesitated to open it. Somehow, facing whatever awaited me became more possible snuggled in the old armchair with Luca and Sam, our aging collie, playing at my feet.

I carefully lifted the seal. Better now than with Antonia here.

> *Dear Lyra,*
>
> *I hope you open this but will understand if I receive no answer. The war has been hard on Papa. He's aging fast.*
>
> *You two were always close, so I felt you should know he hasn't been himself.*
>
> *Mama's as feisty as ever—especially on certain topics. But*
>
> *Papa gets quieter and quieter. If I took Mama to town some-day, would you want to come and visit him? I think it would mean the world.*

Always your Sis,
Suz

My sigh alerted Luca, who glanced my way, but a quick smile mollified him. So strange living relatively close to my parents yet never seeing them.

They could not come to mind without raising a Pandora's Box of questions. Five years it had been since we had spoken. Five long years, but I was still their daughter, and how I missed them.

I thought back to Antonia's comment about love. Could love change this? Could the war?

Papa, slow to speak, had said little when Gabe made known his proposal. Mama, though, let loose. Her tirade included every possible reason against us marrying. Most of these had to do with Roman Catholicism and the need for Methodists like us to steer clear.

For her arguments, Mama even dug back into our French origins—the only time she ever mentioned Papa's family's religion.

"There were good reasons for your father's parents to switch their religion. Jews were being persecuted, even killed.

"But think about it. They might have chosen the Roman church. Why didn't they? Because those Catholics worship graven images— statues of Mary and Joseph and who knows the others?

"You'd have to *sign your children over to the church*. Besides, you can't trust those Italians, don't you know that? They might have connections with the Mafia."

My feeble lack of response only drove her further. But what could I say to change her mind? The Andrettis were people just like us… they worked hard and came through difficulties as immigrants.

Mama's vehemence stunned Gabe. He said he'd never heard of his church taking anyone's children, but otherwise his debating skills flew out the window.

Raw and angry, Mama threatened to send me to one of my older siblings in Texas or California. When she said that, Papa spoke up, and they raised their voices. Seeing nothing could be gained by staying, Gabe went home, and I went to bed.

At that time, my thinking revolved around one concept—*he loved me*. If we had children, they would be *ours*, not just mine. We would make all of these choices together. Though I was young, I knew we loved each other and would for the rest of our lives.

Papa had little influence over Mama, and her decision to shun me brought everyone great pain. The way Mama saw it, they'd done everything they could to rear me as a respectable Protestant girl and failed. Their disappointment only increased when their friends learned what was going on.

Walking down the aisle without Papa, knowing he wanted to be with me, made me ache inside. "With Suzie married, there's just one more trip down the aisle for me," he used to say.

Now, I wondered what he thought as he looked back? Did he wish he had been more forceful? And about the war, did he recall his own service in the last one, his own terrors?

How wonderful it would be to sit with him and talk and to show him Luca and Bella. They'd missed out on knowing the people who brought me into this world.

The last time I spoke with Suzie had not gone well. According to her I had *made my bed and would have to lie in it.*

"You're young and foolish. You've always known how Mama sees Catholics. You brought all of this on yourself."

Had I? Can a person help loving someone? But in Gabe's absence, another question troubled me more. Would my heart ever have mended if I had turned away from him?

Suzie's opened letter trembled in my hand like a baby bird stepping out on a branch to launch its premier flight. I had imagined hearing from her, but not quite yet. For her to contact me meant that Papa must be quite ill.

Out on the road, an automobile door squeaked and Antonia got out. She shut the door and turned back to talk to the driver, probably someone from church who offered her a ride home.

I wished I could speak with someone about Suzie's letter and the decision I had to make, but not Antonia. At least not then. Back when Gabe proposed to me, Antonia had raged back at Mama from a distance.

"What-a your Mamma think? My son, he's-a no good?"

Who, then, to speak to about this? Only Gabe. If only he had been there to help me arrange a secret visit to Papa.

While gathering the eggs, I mulled these questions. My hens hardly stirred when I entered the coop Gabe built for me as a wedding gift.

A chicken coop? Yes, a small building on the property all my own. "And so are these chicks," Gabe had gestured to a wooden-railed crate holding a baker's dozen. "I've seen how important Mama's egg money is, so this is the beginning of yours."

Maybe that was the trouble at my parents' house—no egg money existed. Mama had so little to call her own, especially after our move to Arizona. I had no idea what this step had meant as my first flock grew, pecking the earth around the farm at random.

That first summer, the chickens nested in trees, in the corn crib and milk house, even the barn. When the weather turned cooler, Gabe explained that there could be no more nesting in the barn, for the milk inspector would have been horrified.

Time to gather them up, my flock, and put them in the coop. He brought a waterer and a feeder, disinfected them, and spread fresh sawdust on the floor.

"Now we just have to catch them, Lyralee…this should be fun!" His boy-like grin hardly convinced me, and we spent the next two hours at this task. The hens had no desire to cooperate, to be *cooped-up*, and I couldn't blame them.

That day initiated a conversation between their squawks and my cajoling that has continued ever since. Kind of like a love song, farm style.

"You girls," I began, and they fluttered in their nests. Sometimes what I had to say amounted to more of a monologue, but somehow, I felt they understand what I was trying to communicate… at some level, at least.

There, I would unload my vexations. There, no one else had any idea what I said, and my hens never barked back at me. On the day Suzie's letter came, I went over every word with them, and their small black eyes surveyed me with proper somberness.

Keeping the coop clean had become a number one priority, mostly because chicken poop really stinks. These girls are my responsibility, not that Gabe hasn't helped out at times, but he always has plenty of other chores to do and I enjoy caring for this domain.

The egg truck driver, a medium-sized fellow with a beard and a twinkle in his eye, paid cash per dozen, which I promptly stowed in a jar beneath our bed. Always before, when I worked at the fruit stand, my wages went straight into Mama and Papa's coffers. Not so these earnings—this money belonged to me.

As the years have passed, butchering time has gotten easier, and now I'm used to the routine, but parting with my hens that first year made me sick to my stomach. I didn't taste chicken soup or Antonia's baked chicken for a few weeks.

We'd always butchered at Minnie and Jeb's place, but those hens weren't *ours*. There's a difference. Bella and Luca will understand this and grow up showing prime hens and goats at the county fair, where they'll most likely sell for a good price.

That's a piece missing from my childhood, though we always lived on a farm. Caring for an animal, rearing it, so to speak, and taking pride in your work builds character—I wish we had had the opportunity.

But Mama was new to rural living…Papa had courted her in one of those southern towns next to the army base where he took his training. Before the Great War. Back then, as was true now, girls married beaus they barely knew, only to wave good-bye to them as they deployed to Europe.

When they returned, well…Papa only knew farming, so Mama left her home town and her family. Overnight, she transformed into a farm wife. Sort of.

My wire pail filled fast, and I checked on the children. The house remained quiet, so I headed off to candle the eggs. This might sound like mundane work, but it offered a soothing appeal. A quiet task…solitary labor with time to ponder.

Halfway through the task, I giggled at a memory—Gabe sneaking in behind me once when I was candling. When he poked my sides, I leaped from my stool and cracked several eggs. I'd never quite understood what thrilled him so about surprising someone like this, but he never tried the shenanigan again, at least nowhere near my eggs.

How did we tell Antonia's eggs from mine? For one thing, she kept hers well separated. Besides that, my eggs were a rich, warm brown, and hers were white. And the egg man kept two accounts.

Only during times when I was about to deliver a baby did Gabe take over for me, and I'd always been glad to get back to my hen chores. There was simply something about tending something that belonged to me.

If anything, Antonia was passionate. Passionate about her son coming home, passionate about our packages to help refugees, and passionate about this place. But I had begun to wonder.

Over the past couple of weeks, her hours with the packing committee had extended. Her cooking dwindled…even her famous Italian gravy had gone lacking. Much of the time, the children and I fended for ourselves, eating far less rich fare—probably a healthy diversion. But it wasn't like Antonia to shirk her duties.

Mama had little to work with when we lived in Texas, but always produced a meal for us in the evening. Papa came in at noon to eat, too, and my lunch bag somehow saw me through the day.

I'm grateful that in Mama's kitchen, I learned the basics. Boiling potatoes if nothing else could be found, frying eggs, making pudding from milk, sugar, cornstarch, and eggs. On the days Antonia disappeared, it was easy to fall back into this simple rhythm.

Not much was required to fill a toddler's tummy. As for my own, my girth increased daily, and I'd begun waddling about like the geese that strutted and honked out by the barn.

One day, a visitor stopped by to see Antonia, an old friend who had come and gone over these years. She seemed surprised to find Antonia not at home.

"Hello, Mrs. Spagnoletti. Antonia's at the church, I think, packing boxes. You know about her project, don't you?"

"Mm. But that's only on Tuesdays and Thursdays. I thought she'd be home today for sure."

Tuesdays and Thursdays…that week, Antonia had been gone every single day, and this was Friday. Her friend chatted with Luca a bit, marveling at his vocabulary.

She finally broke away. "Does he ever stop talking?" The answer was obvious, for he continued on even though she moved away.

"He'll be like his father, winning prizes with his tongue, he will."

"We'll see. For now, it's fun to hear his conversations."

"What do you hear from Gabriel?"

My shrug led to her nod. We had all grown weary of saying, "Not much."

"That battle at Anzio's a bitter pill to swallow, I say." Concetta rested her hands on her hips. "I never will understand how those Fascists and Nazis got such a hold on our country. I know times have been hard, but why would good Italians follow someone like Hitler? Can't they see through him?"

Our country—she pronounced those words with tenderness. "Our families still have relatives over there—what must those poor folks be going through right now?"

"Did you know Antonia over there, when you were young?"

Concetta let loose a throaty laugh. "Ah, was I ever young? But to answer your question, no, we met here in the States. My husband got to know Luca out East and they connived together to move here."

"Connived?"

"I would say so. They were full of ambition and willing to take risks. Their parents, both sets, went into shock when we all left. The men had to conspire or their fathers would have put a stop to such goings-on. But our children have been much happier here, away from the big city."

She stared out the window. "I suppose it's a good thing for Antonia to keep busy."

"Oh yes. There's plenty to do around here. Keeping up with everything helps me too."

Concetta frowned and angled her head. "Just how often does she go to the church?"

"Why, lately it's been every day."

"Hmm."

On that mysterious note, Mrs. Spagnoletti called good-bye to Luca and wandered to the drive. Watching her go, I considered how Antonia had been late getting home. Sometimes, the sun had almost set when I heard the vehicle stop at the end of the drive to let her off, and something else had changed.

Was there a lilt to her walk as she descended the driveway? One thing I knew for sure, there was no using asking her about this. She would explain when she was good and ready. Not before.

Chapter Five

Such a short distance. But as the miles rolled by one-by-one, my soul traveled its own private roller-coaster laced with anxiety. Would Suzie's brief note prove true? Did she really take Mama to the bandage-rolling at their church this morning, where the women would eat a potluck lunch afterwards?

Would Mama truly be gone until at least two p.m.?

Without doubt, this amounted to the biggest question. But why would Suzie have made all these plans if she didn't intend to keep them? Knowing there would be no face-to-face with Mama, I could slip in to visit Papa without fear of confrontation.

By the turn into the ranch, I had calmed myself as much as possible. Gabe would have been proud of me facing my own battles. But oh, how I wished he were beside me!

Seeing the small frame house where we lived in my youth, I gasped. Everything looked miniature, even the rose bush beside the front steps. No wonder our older brothers and sisters had left home soon after we moved there. Thinking about them, dubious characters from the past that I barely knew, magnified my smallness. In fact, Gabe knew one of my brothers better than I ever did. As the driver approached the house, I felt small—one insignificant cog in a big family all torn apart. Would I ever see any of them again?

I could see afresh how in comparison to this cottage, Gabe's house once seemed like a mansion. Starting with one room, Luca and Antonia had gradually built a sprawling structure that wandered up and down a hillside.

The first thing I had noticed was that there were places for people to go. You could find private space even inside the house, upstairs if everyone else was on the first floor, or out in the ante-room off the kitchen, perhaps even on the half-cellar stairs if necessary.

If all else failed, you could seek out a stall in the barn, climb the ladder up to the hay mow, or go to the pump house. Had Gabe had this same idea in mind when he decided to build my chicken coop?

We all needed places to go—some would say I meant *to hide*. But secreting yourself away for a time didn't need to be shameful. Sometimes, didn't we all simply long to be unseen?

Having so many possibilities made keeping track of Luca more difficult, I admit. Still, I had always liked the idea of our children growing up with room to be themselves, gaps with no one else around, destinations beyond prying eyes.

Thinking about this as I gathered Luca and Bella from the back seat, I had to shake my head. What kind of space did Gabe have now, confined to tents and trenches? From what we heard in the newscasts, the soldiers dug in at Anzio battled miserable winter cold weather almost as much as they struggled against the Germans.

Somewhere I read that in heavy rains, everything would flood. Then, Anzio nurses had to hold up the instruments and drips going into their patients until they could be moved or some other solution devised. When a cool wind blew here, I thought of them and shuddered.

Gabe never complained in his letters, but he surely must have longed to move about more freely. Always one to take off on a walk or suggest one with me, what must it have been like in such crowded conditions, and the Luftwaffe overhead at any given moment?

When we moved in with his parents after our wedding, we had the upstairs to ourselves, and Antonia and Luca the downstairs—a whole stairwell between the two. The stairwell, in the best of terms, acted as a buffer, and ours even offered a landing where we could pause to peer out one of three windows.

Even now I especially liked the kitchen that rambled on its own, out into a semi-covered stone area for planting herbs and storing pots. There, Antonia hung the nets of garlic she insisted I include in every dish she taught me to make.

In that space, small baskets with stashes of lavender, dried oregano, basil, or a variety of other spices vied for room on the shelves of a tall cupboard. And in enormous pots along the wall stood part of the lavender harvest from last year, lending fragrance and grace.

At my parents' house, I paused before this home with a tacked-on bedroom for Suzie and me. To Mama and Papa, surely it resembled heaven when we arrived, after weeks on the road. When we first moved in, our older brothers and sisters divided the attic for sleeping. Not even one closet in the entire structure.

As I bade our driver good-bye, a neighbor who had errands out this way, we confirmed his intention to come for us at one o'clock. From the corner of my eye, I saw a movement—Minnie, Jeb's wife, out working in her garden. Whatever the season, she found something to do there.

She looked up and gave me a wave, and my hands filled with little ones, I nodded and smiled. Surely now, Papa could do no work for Jeb, but I could not imagine these folks turning my parents out. Minnie hurried my way and grasped my arm.

"Oh, Lyra! How wonderful to see you again! These must be your children? And Suzie has kept me informed about your husband in the Army."

"Yes. I—"

"I'm so glad you came. You'll soon see for yourself, but we're so sad to watch your Papa fade away. What a good man he is. Jeb thinks of him not as a hired man, but as a friend."

She stepped back with a heartfelt twist of her lips. Words failed me, but she understood, gesturing me on toward our house.

When I entered, the rooms seem smashed together, the fireplace running into the same horsehair sofa we always used, and on the other side of the parlor, an overstuffed chair that once welcomed me into its arms. These pieces, here when we came, seemed lavish to us at the time.

In a small bag, sandwiches and fruit for the children swung from my arm, and knocking at the front door, I realized I had brought nothing for Papa. But then I remembered the pictures Antonia took of Luca and Bella a few weeks back. The night before, I had tucked them in my purse.

Just yesterday, they arrived in the mail, photos of the children playing together, and one with Luca in his cowboy hat, riding on Sam. When I asked if I could keep them, her beneficent expression surprised me.

"I'm sending one copy to Gabriel, of course."

"He'll love seeing these. Your pictures mean so much to him."

She didn't even bring up the cost of film and developing, which also surprised me. But then, she had developed a much more placid attitude lately. I attributed this to her work at the church and would bet every penny of my egg money that she headed up that group like a foreman in a factory. Better yet, an Army sergeant.

At any rate, I would leave the pictures with Papa and sneak into Antonia's desk for the negatives to send off for more. I would have to be careful about watching for the package in the mail, but normally she had been leaving before delivery time.

My first knock received no answer. I took a deep breath, and Suzie's note guided me. "He might not hear a knock. Just walk on in."

So I did, somewhat like a mischievous child facing her punishment. How would Papa react? This question had occupied me for days.

In that corner chair I used to enjoy, Papa sat collapsed like a rag doll, eyes closed, breathing so quietly we could not hear. With Luca in my left arm, I pulled Bella inside and caught a whiff of… what, exactly?

"Now we are going to visit Grandpa, Honey."

As we passed the corner cupboard, Luca brushed against something that fell—not much, a pen maybe. But Papa stirred and gave a meager groan.

"Papa?" My heart raced. I cleared my throat. "Papa? It's Lyra, come to see you."

His eyes flew open. Widened. So did his lips, but no words came.

I took the few steps toward him. "I've brought your grandchildren. This is Bella, and this…I want you to meet your grandson, Luca."

"Well." Papa sat up straighter, revealing the outline of his ribcage and the juts of his shoulders. So thin. So fragile.

We hurried to the couch, just a couple of feet from him. At this point, my voice failed me, which might have been a good thing, for Papa reached out his trembling hand to Bella.

"Bapa?" As if magnetized, she moved his way, and he touched her fingers. His eyes filled, and finally my voice cooperated.

"Bella, it's okay. You can sit with Grandpa."

So she did. From my lap, Luca watched without a sound. Luca, quiet? Unbelievable.

Papa began the conversation. "How old are you?"

"I'm five. I go to school now." Such pride in our daughter's tone.

"You do? Such a big girl already."

"Yes. And Luca's only one. He's a little shy."

"Got yourself a smart one here, Lyra." Papa's grin spread as Bella nestled into his side. "Just like you." Hearing him say my name undid me…oh Papa!

Tucked in my arm, Luca soon fell asleep—we looked for moo cows and horses on the way over, so he must have worn himself out. A suffocating sense lined my throat, but I forced myself to speak.

"Papa, you know I never meant to…"

"I know. I know." He drummed his fingers on the armchair. "Your mother…she's a tough one. Keeps her going during hard times, but…"

But. That word opened a vast chasm of emotions.

"Looks like you have another one on the way?"

"Yes. Gabe got a leave in May so it'll be in March, I expect."

"Well." Papa smoothed his fingers over Bella's dimpled elbow.

"I've always wished you and Mama could see… You know Gabe's father died last fall, so these two don't have a Grandpa."

"Hmm."

We sat a while, under the spell of the clock Mama's people brought over on the ship—always time ticking away. Once Gabe and the troops broke through at Anzio, they'd be heading north through Italy and into France, through the country her grandfather left seventy years before.

From Antonia and Luca's homeland to my mother's.

"What do you hear from your soldier boy?"

"Not a lot—he's in the thick of the fighting at Anzio right now."

Papa gestured to the radio. "We listen every night." He shook his head. "Hard to think of them over there. Your mother's praying it'll be over before Suzie's oldest can even think of going."

"She has four children?"

"Mm. The oldest, Cyril, thinks he can change everything over there, him and his friends." Papa let out a long breath. If ever he might mention his own service in the Great War, this would be the time, but Bella had an idea.

"Mommy, is it time to eat?"

"Oh, yes! Here you go." I nudged the bag, and she climbed down to retrieve her food. She sidled back to Papa as if sitting with him had become routine.

"Bapa, Mommy made this for you and me."

Papa carefully took her offering of bread and cheese. "Thank you."

They ate together, and afterward, Bella rested. Had she fallen asleep? Papa did, but she no longer took a nap in the daytime. I shifted Luca's weight to the sofa and wandered to the kitchen. Not much had changed—same curtains and towels, even more threadbare.

In the added-on bedroom, I recalled none of the furniture, scarce as it was. A dresser, the bed Suzie and I once shared, and a small desk and chair.

A sound from the armchair drew me back, and Papa stared at me with a harried look. "Did St. Louis win?"

"You mean in the World Series? They did win one game, four to three."

"'Bout time somebody beat them Yanks… But I heard 'bout Joe DiMaggio's folks—had t' stop fishing 'cause they're Italian. That just ain't right."

"No."

Luca wiggled and started to whimper. "I'm going to change him before our ride comes, Papa."

"Mmm."

I completed the job on the floor near the sofa, and when I returned, Bella sat wide awake, playing *church and steeple* with Papa's fingers. And then our neighbor honked from the driveway.

"Time to go, Bella. Kiss Bapa good-bye."

She tugged Papa's hand, and he rose with difficulty. I thought he was thin before, but now he swayed like a flimsy flag in the wind.

As we left, he patted us all—me on the cheek, Bella and Luca on their heads. I took a deep breath and realized what it was I smelled before—Mama. Every woman's kitchen harbored its own scent.

After we settled in the car, Papa still held onto the screen door handle. Bella waved to him. A sudden wall of regret tumbled over me, and I gasped for air.

Bella, who noticed everything, placed her hand on my arm. "Mama?"

I could not answer her but tried to reassure her with a look. She returned her attention to Luca, and I sank deeper. The swell in my chest, filled with longing for Mama, threatened to devour me.

By the time we reached home, though, I had recovered. Still, an empty sensation caused me to gather the children close.

Chapter Six

Dear Gabe,

Today I saw Papa. I mentioned last time about Suzie contacting me, and together, we made this happen.

Bella sat with him the whole time. You know how energetic she is, but it was as if she realized how weak he is and that she was meant to soak in every moment.

We really didn't talk much, or about much, I should say.

But he let me know he understood I didn't mean to hurt him and Mama when we married.

Without putting it into exact words, we agreed about Mama's… I don't know how to write it. I might say stubbornness about her beliefs. She's always right, and that's all there is to it. I guess I never saw her quite this way.

When you asked me to marry you, I never dreamed what a fuss she would raise! Never could have imagined she would turn on us like she did.

She didn't even try to get to know you—you only came to our house once, to ask for my hand. So it wasn't you she was rejecting, but your heritage. Papa was so quiet that day, but his eyes said more than words, didn't they?

Some questions trouble me. For example, why did Mama allow me to work for a Catholic family? I suppose the answer's pretty clear, though—we needed the money and the vegetables your parents sent home with me. Mama might not have spoken to your parents on the street, but she did accept my wages.

I've never felt I made the wrong decision—not once. You are my one-and-only. I had watched other parents prevent their children from dating or marrying Catholics, but none of this made any sense to me until we were in the middle of it.

One thing I'm sure of. If it had been up to Papa, he would have given us his blessing. I saw this in every movement he made today, heard it in each word from his lips.

I may talk with Suzie some day, since she set up this meeting, but it's pretty certain I won't be meeting with Mama. Papa is so frail, I wonder if I'll ever see him again. At least he was able to meet Bella and Luca. That makes me happy.

Please don't think I'm terribly sad, but besides being my one-and-only, you're my friend. I needed to tell someone about Papa and it surely couldn't have been your mother!

Now for Luca's latest exploits. I believe he's going to become a champion debater like his father—the other day I heard him telling Sam all about the rain outside. Sam looked for all the world like he understood, though Luca's speech is still mostly baby babble.

He rambles on even when he's eating, as if an imaginary buddy is replying. And Bella… maybe by now you have received the photos your mother sent? Your little girl's growing so tall you won't believe it.

She comes home from school with tales as long as the Colorado River. Her teacher calls her "bright and determined" and "just a little bossy."

As the weather cools here, we hear predictions of your progress and pray always for your health and safety. Just so you know, our baby will be familiar with you. Every day I talk to him (I predict a son) and tell him all about you.

Longing for the day you come home to us.

All my love,

Lyra

Luca and Bella romped in the yard, rolling down the hill and struggling up, then falling again. Sunshine embraced us as March aspired to summer's warmth. Lavender buds exuded the merest hint of what was to come, and in the canyon, barren sycamore branches showed yellow. Soon, green leaves would form.

I'd been thinking of this time as dormancy… pulling back and awaiting our third child's birth. A time of growth and undetected change. In many ways, this period would have been idyllic, except for Gabe being so far away.

Soon… soon, the reporters kept saying, until the word had lost its meaning. Soon the battle for Anzio would end. Soon our boys would break free from the German onslaught. I had always thought an onslaught was meant to be carried out and ended quickly, but this one seemed to last forever. From January until now and in the worst possible weather.

My other waiting would soon be over. The baby had lowered, and Antonia asked every morning, "You think today is the day?"

My shrug failed to satisfy her, so she went off about her business. But one day, the seventh, something did seem a bit different. So much time passed between births, I forgot just how it all went with Bella and Luca.

After caring for my hens and gathering eggs, staying close to the house seemed wise, so Luca and I surveyed the lavender plants meandering up and down the rows like gatekeepers for this household.

All appeared well… green had overtaken winter's brown in the stems and branches. No sign of infection. Gabe would be pleased.

Luca pointed to the road and jabbered at a passerby. Ah, Concetta Spagnoletti—it was Tuesday, and she was on her way to the package wrapping.

"Hello! No baby yet?"

"Not yet," I called back. Luca and I walked closer as he added other important information, and Concetta conversed with him.

After she left, we continued our rounds, feeding and petting the goats Antonia milked earlier, sweeping the floor, tidying the kitchen. We ate an early sandwich out in the yard, and when I got up, my water broke.

Luca noticed, of course, and filled me in.

"Let's go inside, Sweetie. Mama's… Mama needs to do something."

With him down for his nap, I considered. A few more hours might pass before the baby came, but Antonia had been getting home so late. If only our area had telephones installed! We kept hearing about this happening, but like Anzio, things moved more slowly than we wished.

I stepped outdoors. The seventh… a good day to be born, since seven was the number of good fortune. Recently, Antonia told me that in Italian lore, the seventh son of the seventh son would be gifted with magical powers.

"Both good and bad," she had added. "So you never know."

Well, we were nowhere near seven. Standing there, a strong pain struck, and I grasped the doorframe. Now what? As I regained my footing, a call sounded from the road—Concetta returning home.

I hailed her… waved for her to stop, and she started toward me. But before she took three steps, another pain hit… stronger.

Now she was running, and we became an instant twosome. "Let's get you inside. Oh my!" She muttered something about Antonia… "That woman… messing around while…"

By then I could do nothing but aim toward the back bedroom, hoping to make it there. Luca snored on the couch and would most likely sleep an hour or so.

Concetta transformed into a self-energized technician, gathering towels and sheets, ordering me to undress, putting water on the stove to boil. All the while, she murmured about Antonia. Antonia being careless, neglectful. Antonia this, Antonia that.

But I was panting so hard, she might have been explaining the intricacies of the solar system for all I knew. Things came back to me—it wouldn't be long before I held a newborn babe in my arms.

How did I know? I couldn't have said for sure. For Bella and

Luca, Gabe had been right there beside me, and he would have remembered all the signs.

"Why-a you not tell me today is the day?" Antonia pointed her accusing finger in my face. "You think I want to miss the birth of my grandson?"

Experience with Mama had taught me the futility of arguing with an enraged woman. The best action was to offer what you could to sooth her.

"Would you like to hold him? He's especially bright-eyed."

Antonia grudgingly extended her arms, and we exchanged this precious weight. She ogled all ten pounds of our strapping little fellow, touched his toes, his ears, his fingers.

"Just like Gabriel."

"Really? Did he weigh so much?"

"No, but otherwise…"

"We've named him after Gabe. It seemed only fitting."

"You and Gabe… you talked this over?" Her eyebrows shot toward the ceiling.

"Of course. We'll call him Gabby, and his middle name comes from my father… Jonathan."

"You're sure about this?"

Her audacity shocked me. This had happened several times since Gabe left, and for once, I talked back. "What do you mean? I am his mother."

She gave me a sideways glance, as if I'd claimed ownership of the whole place. Something in her eyes changed, and I realized that at times, she merely tolerated me for her son's sake. At the same time, I knew we had to live together, and at this point, Gabby was the best I had to offer her.

"Don't you think he's beautiful?"

She could not help but swoon at this miracle in her arms, and I knew her anger was mostly at herself. What she was doing mattered not at all to me. She was here, the one grandparent blessed to hold this child, and we had to work together.

She drummed her fingers on the wooden arm of her chair and softened before my very eyes. What made it so difficult for that generation of women to say they were sorry? To express regret for their actions or even to explain what had been going on?

Who knew? We sat there much longer with Antonia asking if I had shown Gabriel to Luca and Bella.

Indeed! This afternoon, Concetta made a perfect fill-in for Grandma, cooking dinner for us, taking Luca along to fetch Bella from school and bringing the children in to see their new brother.

Oh, the excitement, the wonder in their eyes! Then Concetta brought me toast with lavender honey… my, what a delight. I basked in the memory without laying out the details for Antonia.

All I could think of was how it would be when Gabe first saw this child, his namesake. What a day that would be for us all!

Chapter Seven

Antonia stood as a testimony to willfulness. She had started spending most of Monday, Wednesday, and Friday at home. On Tuesday and Thursday, she added my egg chores to hers before she left.

Several times in those first days since Gabby's birth, I felt certain she would tell me where she had spent her time over the past weeks. She reported to me on the number of packages sent, the people who helped, and the weather, but could not bring herself to say anything else.

In the end, the information came via Concetta, who visited often now and loved rocking Gabby to sleep. Antonia accepted this with better humor than I might have thought.

One afternoon I was about to put Luca down for his nap when Concetta confided the news. "Do you know Antonia has a beau?"

"A…? She what?" I could not have been more thunderstruck.

"Remember the family that moved in down the road? The man who brought his wife and children here to be with family while he was deployed?"

"Yes."

"He brought his father-in-law, too." She emphasized *father-in-law* and waited for me to comprehend.

"His father-in-law… Yes, I think I met him briefly, right at the first. He's from Mexico?"

"His name is Bernardo, and he's a natural-born carpenter. He began fixing things around the church, and when Antonia started working with the packages… Well, you know how things like this begin. She misses Luca, and Bernardo's lonely too. His wife died a couple of years ago."

"Ah."

"Antonia and I have been friends for a long time. I love her, but no one could ever be more stubborn. We have had to stay away from each other for periods, when I have gone against what she wished. I always know when I need a vacation from her, but we always come back together."

Concetta placed Gabby in his cradle and pushed it back and forth with her bare toes. A lovely rhythm, this—so soothing. Meanwhile, Luca slept blissfully in my arms—I had no energy to move him. Gradually, I allowed an image of Antonia and a handsome, bronze-skinned man to enter my consciousness.

"Did she ask you to tell me?"

"No." Concetta peered into my eyes as a fortune teller might. "But I believe she wanted me to."

So it was, a week after Concetta's revelation, that Antonia arrived home one day bringing Bella from school. But she did not come solo. A tall, bronzed man stood beside her in the kitchen, removing his work hat and tapping the wooden planks with one boot toe.

Her high cheekbones radiated the hue of sumac leaves in autumn—she looked truly beautiful. Her tone seemed normal, level.

"Lyra, have you met Bernardo?" She called to me as I rocked Gabby, and I wondered why she came no closer.

"Maybe when you first moved here?" I shook Bernardo's hand after he crossed the space between us. "Good to see you again."

He smiled and nodded at Gabby, asleep in his crib. "Such a strong Niño you have!" He returned to Antonia, who had not moved. "Now, where is that fence that needs a new post?"

They went outside, and I considered myself *told*. From now on, Bernardo, perhaps in his mid-fifties, would come and go and become part of our family. Many nights he would eat dinner with us and listen to the war news before leaving. Sometimes, one of the children would fall asleep in his arms.

June had come—one full year since I last saw Gabe. That evening, Bella asked for Daddy's Bee Story.

"You remember Bentley Bee?"

Antonia made a *bzzzz* sound, flying her fingers around Luca and landing under his neck. His giggles set us all laughing, and Bella demanded, "Tell us the Bee Story!"

So I gave my best rendition of Gabe's tale, how Bentley Bee crossed the Atlantic in a skep with the Jamestown Colonists, broke free from the hive one day and entered the deep Virginia woods. I raised my eyebrows like Gabe would have, to show there had been some danger involved.

"He found a new home in the hollow of a soft maple tree, but soon began to feel lonely. And then, wouldn't you know, he heard a *bzzzzzing* somewhere outside. He went out to check and found not one, but a whole *lot* of bees swarming nearby.

"'Come over here,'" he called to them. "'I've found a perfect place for us to make a hive.'"

"So the other bees followed him and they created a new community."

Bella's eyes had gotten heavy, and Luca had left us for slumberland. If they had been alert, I could have gone on, for Gabe's stories never really ended. Bentley Bee and his family enjoyed making wonderful honey, but one day, a little girl named Bella entered the wood with her father.

He moved the hive to a field full of flowers—surely lavender must have been amongst those early crops—and the amount of nectar increased the bees' production while pollinating the entire field. Everybody was happy—the bees content to do their work, the colonists thrilled with abundant honey.

As far as I could recall, Gabe told this story to Bella only a few times around Thanksgiving of '41. But she still remembered.

April passed, and May followed like an obedient servant. One evening we finally heard something positive from the Mediterranean front.

The final push at Anzio began with May twenty-third's Allied artillery barrage on the Cisterna front. It met with stiff resistance along the entire line from Carano to the Mussolini Canal. But by evening, our First Special Service Force and First Armored Division had breached the main line of enemy resistance.

The next day, the Sixth Corps cut Highway Seven above Cisterna and encircled the town. Finally, on May 25, through heavy fighting that resulted in great losses, Cisterna fell.

Earlier that day, the Ninety-first Reconnaissance Squadron, 85th Infantry Division, U.S. II Corps raced north from Terracina across the Pontine Marshes to meet soldiers of the 1st Battalion, 36th Engineer Combat Regiment from the Anzio beachhead.

At last, we celebrate this link-up between Fifth Army forces.

How long have we planned for this! How long have we awaited the day when we can say with finality, "The Anzio beachhead is no more!"

The breakout toward the west proved costly, with the First Armored Division losing one hundred armored vehicles in the first day alone and suffering over four thousand casualties in the first five days. However, our boys took nearly five thousand enemy prisoners and destroyed or damaged almost three thousand enemy vehicles.

The result of all this? Let us shout the grand news from the rooftops! At last, Rome lies in Allied hands on this day, the fourth of June, 1944.

Antonia clapped her hands but frowned. "They didn't mention the Forty-fifth Infantry at all."

"Thirty-six thousand American troops are fighting there—thirty-six thousand! Maybe your son's unit got a rest this time. They have been in battle so long and have taken many attacks. My nephew from Colorado is with the Forty-fifth, too. We haven't heard from him since February."

Grateful for Bernardo's common-sense input, I gave thanks for his gentle presence in our household. Now that the secret was out, our routine had found a quieter rhythm. With all there was to do, I appreciated his work out in the fields and the way he often noticed what needed to be done before Antonia or I mentioned it.

The war kept changing things. In this instance, both at Anzio and here, the change seemed good. After the report, Antonia got out a map of Italy and France, spread it on the table and showed us how far our troops still had to travel before they reached Germany.

Bella traced the route with her finger.

To me, it looked like a long, long way.

After everyone slept, I crept downstairs and out into the anteroom. Something about this place—probably its scents—invited me to breathe deeper, to relax.

Thinking about Antonia and Bernardo's newfound romance and about the look in Concetta's eyes when she broke the news, I marveled at their long friendship. To know someone so well, understand their faults, and yet remain faithful amounted to true loyalty.

A breeze swept through the window as I sank on Antonia's stone bench and leaned against the cool wall. The news of Rome being taken lightened my heart… Would Gabe see that ancient city? But this victory came at such great cost and through terrible suffering.

Suddenly it seemed Gabe was right beside me. He had come home from college for Christmas and was telling me about the naming of Phoenix… that a confederate soldier wanted to name it Stonewall, after Stonewall Jackson. Others suggested Salina, but then another man put forth *Phoenix*.

"Why? Because the city rose out of ashes, like the mythological bird. The ancient Hohokam civilization used to thrive right where Phoenix grew up."

The breeze rustled a bit stronger, rattling a shutter. Something about this memory strengthened me. In the same way Phoenix conquered the salt water, the desert, and other challenges to become a city in its own right, our troops had climbed out of the muddy rubble of Anzio.

The sensation of Gabe being so close lasted only a few moments but made my spine tingle. He was doing his work—what he wanted to do, and until he came home, I must do the same.

Gabby—what a chunky, happy baby! His name fit him perfectly. He was like a waterfall, steadily generating charm. Those dark eyes of his drew people in just like Gabe's, and his chin folded into a myriad of dimples when he smiled.

Nearly six months old, he seemed even more good-natured than Bella and Luca had been at the same age. Of course, he absorbed their energy and had their antics to applaud, their grins and noises to mimic.

Summer was in full swing, and August brought the corn harvest. That work was so much easier with Bernardo there. Antonia worked alongside him when she could, and their bond was obvious. I kept thinking they would announce the date of their marriage, but not yet.

All through June and July, as the news turned almost solely to the Normandy Invasion and our troops battling through the hedgerows of Northern France, Antonia fussed that we hadn't heard from Gabriel. Her forehead wore thunderclouds poised to burst.

What was there to say? Of course, not hearing from Gabe bothered me too—kept me awake at night. If the worst was over in Italy, why did he not write? But since Antonia displayed her feelings so strongly, how could it possibly help to add mine?

Better to retreat upstairs to bed after the children were sleeping.

Prayers, prayers, prayers—if only I knew what to pray! The theme of one Sunday sermon helped… God knows our thoughts and desires. Beyond our wildest imaginations, He is able to answer our prayers even before they mount to heaven.

Why pray, then? The theory was that prayer might be designed for *our benefit,* to help us put into words our hidden fears and qualms, to provide an emotional release.

So I kept up my woebegone attempts, although the sight of deceased soldiers' names on the newspaper rolls taunted me. Those lists, ever growing, stopped all words in my throat, but I wrote them to Gabe later.

Oh Gabe, how glad I am for our lavender field! Harvesting has helped me through the hotter months. Ooh, the comforting scent of so many blossoms in one place. Antonia has begun to run the distiller you made, and I think of European doctors using this balm for healing wounds.

Sometimes I watched Antonia at work out in the shed. Focused completely on the process, she heated the lavender with rain water in a pressure cooker on a hot plate. We had harvested what she needed the night before and let the branches wilt overnight—this shocking produced a better quality of oil.

As steam passed through the herbs into the head space Antonia left at the top of the pot, it expanded and rose into a delicate glass instrument fitted to the cooker. I didn't pretend to understand the entire process, but as the steam and oil rose, the water fell and tiny glass fingers inside the glass tube captured the oil.

What a time-consuming method, but it worked. Drop by drop, the amount of oil increased until we had enough to make small vials of medicines—an ointment for headaches, one to put on the children's cuts, drops to ease insomnia, and others.

And all because of Gabe's love of lavender.

Have you been wounded, my Gabriel? In my best moments I picture you unscathed, crossing the land north of Rome with angels around you. These musings, I kept to myself.

Right now lavender's fragrant essence was soothing the ragged edges of my tension and anxiety—wounds in themselves. I spent as much morning time as possible outdoors, giving Bella and Luca child-sized tasks to perform.

The small wagon Gabe played with as a child became their constant companion. I conjured loads for them to carry to and from the shed to the barn, the barn to the house, and soon they envisioned their own cargos.

"Here, take this pile of twigs over to Bernardo. He will know what to do with them." Knowing children, he entered this game without questions, understanding the need to keep them busy.

After naps and dinner, we went out again. The perfume called to us, and later, I placed small packets under our pillows. By the time Bernardo hugged Bella, Gabby, and Luca good-night and chugged off in his rattletrap pick-up, weariness overtook us and the sweet scent welcomed us to bed.

No time now for Antonia to catch my ear, for I fell asleep with my babies… if I slept at all.

So midsummer passed, but then we heard that someone local has lost a family member in the fighting. I knew the family name, that is all, and submerged a wild desire to run to them and ask how much time passed before they discovered the truth.

Of course, Antonia nearly burst with the details, but Bernardo calmed her until after the children were asleep. The Simmons boy had died, a casualty of the Pacific front. A double amputee, she said, he might have made it home, but fragments too deep for the doctors to remove caused infection.

I could barely hear her out. Nausea overtook me, and I fled up the stairs. The landing gave me pause between the horrors of war and my babies. A few deep breaths, a prayer for the family to make it through, and another for Gabe.

During those days, this young man's family hovered close to my heart. With every prayer for them, I pled for Gabe and his buddies.

One morning I awoke thinking I needed to take Gabby to

see Papa, since several months had passed since our visit. I wrote Suzie a quick note, hoping we could arrange another meeting. Her immediate reply startled me.

As I write, Papa is passing from this world. You might try to come, but he won't recognize the children, and possibly not you. Sometimes he seems to know who I am, but most of the time he has no idea. The other thing—Mama refuses to leave his side. Not for one moment.

Even so, do you want to see him again?

My instinctive answer? Yes. But after considering the possible effects of showing up—Mama going into a rage, disturbing Papa, setting whoever else might be visiting on edge—my answer could only be *No.*

Something had grown in me during these long months, especially since that precious time the children and I spent with Papa. Some might call it dignity, self-confidence, or the good kind of pride.

Having eight children took so much energy, and Mama was tired by the time I came along. Maybe she had tried everything she knew to avoid pregnancy but failed. I did feel for her, but I still came into this world with needs and gifts.

To be unwanted also required energy. As a human being, I deserved better. I knew this in my soul. An infant could not help being born, however disillusioned with parenthood her mother had been.

If sweet Gabby were my eighth child, would I have felt the same as Mama did about me? This I asked to be fair, even though there was no definitive answer. In my bones, no matter what, I know I would still have loved this cheerful little fellow.

As I considered all of this, from somewhere—probably Miss Tennyson's English class—arose portions of a poem called the *Desiderata.* I still recalled the warmth I felt when I first read its words.

"You are a child of the Universe, no less than the trees and the stars. You have a right to be here…"

On the porch, I rehearsed Suzie's note. She said nothing about what she thought best, but her sentiments echoed between the lines.

You have your memories of Papa and were able to visit him. Why cause trouble at this point? Why not let him enter eternity at peace?

The decision became easy. My visit had highlighted the assurance of Papa's love, and I had no need to prove mine for him.

Chapter Eight

Just when *normal* had re-established itself in our household, the telegram arrived. Antonia had gone to town that morning, so I grabbed Luca and clutched him to my chest as I opened the door.

"Telegram, Ma'am. If you would sign right here, please."

My scratchy signature matched my throat. Queasiness overtook me as I lowered onto the couch. For some time, I stared at objects in the room… the sewing machine where it seemed I had spent half my life, the cupboard, kept relatively tidy but in constant use. Even from where I sat, some spills and stains showed.

Antonia's three iron skillets and her huge soup pot, always at the ready above the stove, her straw broom, also available at a moment's notice. The dishes lining the shelves, the stack of clean handkerchiefs Antonia kept beside the door for Bernardo, the clock's hands, ever moving onward, never at rest.

Foolish me. Since Gabe left, I had wished for time to flee faster, and now it had brought me to this juncture. Suspended between what was and what would be, I faltered. The message I held might change everything.

Everything? No, I reasoned. No words on paper could change my love for Gabe or for our children. No missive, no matter how dire its contents, would alter what my senses told me, if I gave them a chance.

The scent from the anteroom—sage and creeping thyme and dill laced with lavender—bespoke healing and care about the little things, the spices of life. From outdoors, Bernardo's hammer clanging against iron added another dimension, and a cow's moo reminded me of our stable barn and my hens clucking nearby in their coop.

None of these things would dissolve if I read this telegram. No, their very presence would sustain me through whatever was to come.

Luca crawled down and fixed dark eyes on me. "Baby wake," he announced, but he said this ten times during Gabby's naps. He loved his brother, sometimes a bit too much, poking at Gabby's fat cheeks, tugging on his hand as if he might lengthen his arms, pulling at his legs as if to strengthen them so he could run and play.

"No, honey. He needs his sleep. You play with Sam."

His startled look recapped our house rules. We never had allowed Luca to go outside alone—not yet. I amended my words. "You can go out just this once. But only this one time and stay near the door. I'll be watching."

Forehead creased in puzzlement, Luca let himself out the screen door like a big boy and carefully pulled it shut. Suddenly he had risen to Bella's level. Such a minute difference in his world, yet significant. Except for the telegram, this milestone never would have happened so soon, and he seemed to realize the significance.

A thousand thoughts waged war inside my head. Gabby and Luca would be the sole males to carry Gabe's legacy if—

No. No! I *would not* think this way! Hadn't up to this point, so why should I now? There was no reason to claim the worst thought that reeled through my mind.

A long breath. Another. A glance out at Luca, who had proceeded perhaps three steps from the door. The old couch covering, once soft velvet, scratched at my palm. This could not wait forever.

The tearing sounded too loud, as if my soul were being rent in two. I sucked in a breath and read.

REGRET TO INFORM YOU YOUR HUSBAND STAFF SERGEANT GABRIEL L ANDRETTI WAS SLIGHTLY WOUNDED IN ACTION TWENTY MARCH IN ITALY. SERGEANT ANDRETTI IS NOW

ABOARD A U.S. ARMY HOSPITAL SHIP. YOU WILL BE ADVISED AS REPORTS OF CONDITION ARE RECEIVED.

"He's alive!" This was all I could manage. Miss Tennyson, who loved ancient literature, used to say, "Theocritis, a Greek poet, wrote, *While there's life there's hope, and only the dead have none.*"

So we had hope. With this foundation, I scrutinized the wording.

Who had any clue what the Army meant by *slightly*? If they chose the correct adjective, surely we wouldn't have needed to be notified, and Gabe would have been sent back to the line long ago.

But he remained alive. This was all that mattered.

"Wounded in March?! How can it be that we only hear now?" As I expected, Antonia's reaction differed from mine. Thankfully, Bernardo had stayed to eat with us that night. He patted her shoulder.

"This is the way of war. So many casualties, we cannot expect—"

Antonia cut him off. "But five months. Surely it cannot take that long to write a simple telegram."

"Ah, but they have so many men wounded. So many families to write." Perhaps hearing my relieved sigh, Bernardo guided Antonia to the couch. "Military operations get disorganized—everything takes longer than it should."

Antonia burst out. "But how can we find out how badly he is hurt? How can we know where that ship is, or if decent doctors are there?"

Bernardo's wince showed even from a distance. "We can't. The chances are, by now he has been moved to a hospital somewhere in the States. We have to trust."

"Trust!" Antonia leaped up and paced the room. Luca grabbed at her skirt, but she shook him off before wrenching open the door and disappearing into the twilight.

Bernardo glanced my way. His shrug communicated his vexation.

"No need to upset them." He gestured to the children. "Let's give her some time alone out there."

"Nonna… outside?" Luca's face screwed up as if he might wail, so I grabbed him and Bella. "Bernardo, could you please keep an eye on Gabby while I bathe these two and tuck them in?"

"*Si.*" Bernardo grinned. "Maybe that will give Toni enough time to cool down."

"*Toni…*" The nickname sounded much too casual for Antonia, too easy, too flippant, too… young. But the softness of Bernardo's eyes testified of his love for her.

That day initiated the game of wanting another telegram, yet not wanting one. Ambiguity, I found, can be dreadful to endure, like walking in heavy fog. The haziness obscured all that was normal, removing the certainty we usually felt about our surroundings. Our minds filled with doubts.

Shouldn't we have come to the turn we sought by now, or had we passed it? No… perhaps a bit farther. Oh, for the heavy mist to lift and for the light of certainly to return!

Through the next weeks, I stumbled through, and all of a sudden, the end of September arrived. Against the deep rust of sumac, Bella danced to school in the mornings and waltzed home in the afternoons, full of facts and stories. Daily, Luca grieved her leaving him behind for another life apart from him, but not for long.

That busy boy kept me alert every second. He flirted with his baby brother until Gabby fell asleep. Then he marched to the end of the lavender field—his limit—to watch Bernardo out harvesting the corn with his steel pick.

Bang! Slap! Crunch! The clattery chorus repeated, with Luca mocking Bernardo's every move. I could almost trust him to stay where I told him to… but *almost* does not equal surety. In a twinkle, he could be gone, racing down the road to search for his sister.

The magical change would come, when trustworthiness would alight in his eyes. This happened with Bella and would with Luca, but in the meantime, I stayed on the alert.

As each ear of corn fell into the back of Bernardo's truck, my heart swelled with gratitude. This man worked as hard as any ant struggling up and down the trail to her hill with heavy loads on her back. As far as I know, he received no pay.

We ground the ears for feed in our portable grinder, a job designed to build muscles. Sometimes Bernardo took the handle from me, saying, "*Es el trabajo para mi.*" His work, not mine.

He came and went like sunshine and shadows, asking for nothing but accepting what we offered. That amounted to glasses of cold lavender tea, sandwiches, Antonia's sublime *biscotto,* and the evening meal.

Sometimes I wondered what it was about her that attracted him, besides her natural beauty, for this waiting period had coarsened her. Her smile became a unique occurrence, appearing only once in a great while, like an eclipse to be observed and celebrated. Her forefinger waggled more often these days, never in true fury at the children, but I kept watch.

The rapport between Bernardo and her reminded me that opposites often carry a special appeal. Bernardo, quiet and unassuming, never one to raise his voice, and Antonia… well, you know.

"Mama may be sharp sometimes—she doesn't always watch her words, but she means well," Gabe once warned me. But this was different, like a bitter streak in a grapefruit. I sometimes wondered if when Gabe returned, he would find his mother barely recognizable.

As an example, some days before the news carried this report.

Operation Market Garden begins today. Allied paratroopers have landed in the Netherlands and XXX Corps has advanced from Belgium. The Battle of Arnhem has begun in the Netherlands and the 3rd Canadian Division has begun Operation Wellhit to take the fortified town of Boulogne in northern France.

Since the collapse and mass retreat of German forces in August, our troops have advanced headlong across the River Seine and into Belgium and Eastern France. With the Free French, American Forces captured Paris with little effort, and early this month, the pursuit halted so formations could be replenished and refueled.

Allied armies stand, British and Canadians to the north of the German Reich, Americans to the south, and deliberations began concerning logistics.

The plan to take Germany begins in the north, with a narrow thrust through the Netherlands into the Ruhr Valley, Germany's prime industrial heartland. All three divisions of the First Allied Airborne Army are being employed.

The US 101st Division will capture Eindhoven and bridges over the canals and rivers north of the town. The US 82nd Division is tasked with securing crossings in and around Nijmegen, and holding the strategically important Groesbeek Heights to the east, which border German territory around Kleve.

Finally taken, the bridge over the lower Rhine at Arnhem is designated for the British First Airborne Division with the First Polish Independent Parachute Brigade attached. Once again, we send heartfelt wishes and prayers for a speedy end to this war.

"Market Garden! Wellhit! *Dio Mio*! Why do our commanders take so long to make decisions? Don't they know what to do?" Antonia's eruption ascended like steam from her cooking pot. "Why don't we just go and *get* those Germans? Can it be that hard? Why don't we just rip out their throats?"

At times like that, I took refuge in silence. Nothing I could have possibly have said would have made even a tiny bit of difference.

Bernardo raised an eyebrow toward me. I would describe what happened next, but at that precise moment, someone knocked at the door.

Still in full daylight, I recognized the dreaded—and hoped-for—uniform. The telegram delivery man had set foot on our stoop again.

Antonia became aware and rushed past me toward the door. For once, I was glad for her impatience. I propped myself against the wall—glad for her to open this one.

With bowed shoulders, Antonia turned my way. "For you."

I nodded. "Go ahead—you open it."

Bernardo hurried to Antonia's side, and the children instinctively stopped what they were doing. Antonia read in silence, her face a well-worn hardscrabble path.

Struck dumb except for one emission, "*Madonna!*" she handed the note to Bernardo, who brought it to me. I read the words aloud, each detached from the other yet part of a whole, like petals on a rose.

> ... RECUPERATING FROM WOUNDS ... FORT SAM HOUSTON CONVALESCENT HOSPITAL. ON OR AFTER OCTOBER 15 ... SPOUSAL VISITS ALLOWED

Grasping Bernardo's hand, Antonia collapsed against him.

He supported her while twisting toward me.

"You must go to him. We will watch *los niños* for you."

The armchair, Gabe's favorite spot, caught me. Bella and Luca climbed up. Oh, the scent of their hair, the softness of their skin. I could have lost myself in their small persons.

"Mama… what does it say?" Bella had begun reading words and stood in awe of ink on paper.

As in a dream, I whispered. "Daddy's getting better."

The clock took over as Bernardo guided Antonia to the couch. Her tears flowed like a fountain, and I understood. She was a mother—it was just that her fears emerge shaped like wrath.

"Yes. Daddy's getting better. He's been hurt in the war, but he'll be all right."

When I recovered a bit more, I added more details. "Daddy is in a hospital in Texas, and the doctors are taking care of him."

"Texas—Daddy said the bees found a new grove there!"

"Don't you remember Bea, our oldest sister?" Suzie perched on the couch as if she visited every day. Having her here, sitting right beside me, brought back an avalanche of memories.

On the floor between us, Luca rested with his head on a snoozing Sam. Buddies forever.

"The one who stayed in Texas when we left? She was already married then, right?"

"She's the one. She lives in San Antonio, close to the army hospital, and her daughter's a nurse there. She has three other children, all nearly grown, of course. When I told her about Gabe being there and you coming to see him, she let out a whoop.

"'My baby sister! I can't believe she's married, with children of her own.'"

"You called her?"

"We can make calls from the Mercantile now, haven't you heard?"

"No. We hardly ever need anything from town, so..."

"Hmm. Anyway, a call costs a dime. You do live an isolated life. I heard on the Merc grapevine that some soldier from here had been taken to a hospital in San Antonio and put two and two together. Figured it just might be Gabe. You're surely going to visit him, aren't you?"

"Well, I..." My head swam with possibilities. Suzie was right. I *did* live an isolated life here. Since I made our clothes and we grew so much of our food the Mercantile had little to offer, and the grapevine held no interest for me, especially with Antonia's personal grapevine in action.

Most of my former classmates had joined up to fight or moved down to Phoenix to work in war industries. Their wives, including the few girls I knew in school, had left their children with grandparents to build airplanes somewhere, make bombs, or pack parachutes.

Anybody could be a *Rosie the Riveter* these days. I doubted that anybody else I knew stayed around here once the call came for workers.

Ten minutes ago, Suzie had parked a grey Studebaker in our driveway and there she stood, giving me a look that said she was taking charge. Good thing Antonia had left for the church before she drove in, or we might have had a conflict of commanders.

"Of course you're going to see Gabe. Want me to watch your little ones?"

"It makes more sense for them to stay here at home with Antonia, but thank you anyway."

"Bea says you can stay with her. It's only a ten-minute walk to the new hospital from her house. And would you believe her husband headed up the masonry crew that built the place?"

The thought of digging out my eggy money, buying tickets, packing a suitcase, and boarding a train for such a long trip set my head buzzing. But none of this seemed to frazzle Suzie, who angled her head and squinted at me.

"You ought to get out more. And you need to get used to having family again."

"I guess so." She couldn't have been more right, but after all those years, seeing Bea would be like meeting a stranger for the first time. I pictured her looking like Mama, but really had no idea.

"Once you get your ticket, we'll give her another call so she can meet you at the station."

"But I don't even know what she looks like."

"Silly, that's what pictures and letters are for. We've got a few weeks to get you all set. I think I'll order a flyer from the South Pacific Railroad Office so you can read up on everything—then you'll be prepared. I'll bring it over when it gets here."

She got up to leave but turned back at the door. "And just in case you're worried about Mama finding out, don't waste your time. She's so upset over losing Papa, she doesn't have any room for anything or anybody else. I guarantee she won't know a thing about this."

She opened the door but paused again. "And I'm taking you shopping next week. Pick your day, morning or afternoon. You need a new dress."

"I can sew one up in a jiffy."

"Nope, this is a landmark trip you'll be taking. This dress has to be store-bought, little sis."

Chapter Nine

Brooke Army Medical Center. A brand-new building named after the General who supervised its construction. I had never seen such an enormous building, much less gone into one, and somewhere in there, behind one of those windows, lay Gabe.

Cement stairs led me through tall double doors into a foyer, and according to a flyer I found there, this facility boasted the latest technology, a superior medical staff, and nearly five hundred beds. A silver-haired lady in an impeccable white blouse and grey suit beckoned me to the information booth.

She turned to me and explained that those figures had changed in recent months. Now this hospital had more than a thousand beds, and soon that number would increase.

"Are you here to visit someone?" Her kindly eyes, grey with just a hint of green, made me think of Bea, who walked me over that morning and offered to come inside. But I knew she had work to do and worried about her son Cyril constantly. At nearly seventeen, he threatened to lie about his age and enlist.

"Quite a few of his friends have already. I wouldn't be surprised at all, and if he does insist on going early, Joe and I will sign for him. But it won't be easy."

Around midnight the night before, voices had awakened me—an argument. And one of the phrases that stuck with me this morning went something like: "But this is *my* war—if I wait too long, it'll all be over!"

So that morning, seeing Bea's bloodshot eyes, I told her I'd be fine. She'd already gone out of her way to meet me at the train station and settle me in a spare bedroom used as a sun porch in the summer months. Now it was perfect, with an evening breeze made for sleeping.

Except that sleep came hard.

The night before such an auspicious day, how could anyone sleep?

I had sat by the window from midnight until three, realizing Gabe's nearness. My questions churned like a Texas tornado—could he sleep? Did he have pain? A hundred others ran through my mind.

Antonia had another fit when Bea wrote to answer Suzie's question about Gabe's condition. "Our daughter works in a different part of the hospital entirely. She did try to find out something, but she's not allowed to talk about patients outside the hospital."

"Why don't they tell you? Don't you have a right to know? After all, you're his wife. Gabe could have a broken leg, or maybe the fighting drove him loco. Who can know?"

Bernardo to the rescue once more. "Just think of all the patients there, and so many more being sent home wounded every day. It's all they can do, I think, to meet their needs."

The night before I left, Bernardo made an announcement. "Antonia and I will marry soon."

Suddenly shy, Antonia clasped his hand. "Bernardo has been building us a house on the old Wilson property down the road. By the time Gabe gets home, it may be ready."

There it was, complete with a timeline. So much change was going on. Another big transformation for Gabe to adjust to.

After attempting to sleep again last night, I got up to creep around the house. From Bea's back porch, the top floor of the hospital showed in the distance. Lights on all night… nurses always on duty. Like Gabe said, he was one small bee in a hive.

Somewhere inside, a door closed, and soon Bea stood beside me.

"I can't sleep either. I imagine you're all pins and needles. I sure would be."

"I wish this were over… our first meeting, I mean."

"Yes. And it will be soon. I'm glad you came—seeing you will mean the world to Gabe, I'm sure."

"I can't thank you enough for letting me…"

"Why, we're sisters. I've always regretted how our family got ripped apart, always wondered about you. If it weren't for Suzie…"

"Yes. She's been so helpful. If it hadn't been for her, I wouldn't have been able to see Papa before he died."

"And that was good?"

"Oh yes. I left with so much more than when I came. He was weak already, but our talk filled in some holes."

"Ah. Those holes… I've got them too. I wish I could feel closer to Mama."

"You do?"

"Sure. There's a reason we never made the trip out there to see them." In faint moonlight, Bea's profile reminded me of Mama's. "Hey, shall we try for a few more hours before morning?"

I followed Bea into the house and did fall asleep for a while. Somehow, it helped to know she felt distant from Mama, too.

A few hours later, there I was, at the hospital. I asked the information clerk where I could find Gabe. She flipped pages in a thick notebook and located his name. "Room 267, dear. But visiting hours don't begin until one this afternoon."

"Ah. Thank you." *So disheartening.* I left the foyer, but then thought, *Why not walk up to second floor? At least this part would be familiar when I come back.* I did this, turned around, and returned to the entrance.

Outside, Bea stood not far away, chatting with someone on the circular drive. She hailed me and grabbed my arm when I neared.

"Eleanor, meet my baby sis! She's here to visit her husband, back from the Italian Campaign."

We talked for a while, and on the walk back to Bea's, met someone else she knew. Another brief exchange, and we were soon climbing her front stairs.

"Well, we have the whole morning, then. How about we go shopping?"

"Shopping?"

"You probably don't get to do a lot of that back home."

"No, but…"

"We can just window shop, but I do need a new pair of shoes. Looks like you could use a pair, too."

My scuffed toes and loose soles testified to that. I thought how wonderful my new dress felt—the one Suzie insisted on buying me for the trip, but new shoes seemed like too much luxury.

"Maybe."

"Fifteen minutes for this first time, Ma'am." The nurse touched the handle of the craft room door, and a big red boulder toppled down my throat. "Can you tell me anything at all about Gabe's condition?"

She peered at me as though measuring my strength. "The fighting he was in when he was wounded went on for days. When he arrived at the hospital ship, the field docs had bandaged him up, and he had to board by stretcher. The prognosis was that he never would walk again.

"He must have been determined, because now he can, although his right leg still drags a little. And the surgeons had to leave some shrapnel in his head—too dangerous to try to remove."

My heart raced. "What does that mean?"

"Like many other patients here, he has a stutter, and is having to gradually re-learn some things. That's why we bring him down here every afternoon, plus it's a good place to re-unite with family for the first time—better than the ward.

"You can see he's working with a puzzle right now. Hopefully the movements he's making will strengthen his arm muscles."

"He was wounded there, too? How many…"

"Ma'am, between the shrapnel and the actual bullets, it appears he suffered three serious wounds."

Gabe at work. On a puzzle. He'd never liked doing them, but through the small window, it was clear that he was totally engaged.

"All right? Are you ready?"

"Yes, thank you so much."

The closer I moved, the tighter I clutched my purse. This fellow bent over a child's puzzle bore little resemblance to my strong Gabe. Gabe, who could create anything he desired—a chicken coop for me, a pull toy for a child, a homemade still to turn lavender buds into oil.

This fellow, so thin and haggard looking, with trembling fingers—could this truly be Gabriel Andretti? He kept his head bent as I approached.

My new shoes squeaked, but he seemed not to notice. Bea found a pair in the same store, and at a two-for-one price, was thrilled. She paid the bill, saying they would come to visit us some day and make up for it.

When I protested, she grabbed my hand and said, "This is all of the birthday presents you didn't get from me as you were growing up, sis."

Thinking of the sincerity in her expression, and now seeing Gabe, my eyes smarted. But I glanced around at other wives or girlfriends with their soldiers, some of them with arms or legs missing, some with blank stares, lost in another world.

"This *is* Gabe. He *will* heal, and I will do whatever I can to help."

When I slipped into a chair beside him, he looked up. His face drained of color and his eyes filled. His lips moved, but no words issued forth.

"Gabe? It's me."

"L-lyra.... M-m-my Lyralee." He attempted a smile, but his muscles didn't all cooperate. He took my hand. "You came."

"Surely I did! I would've come sooner, but they said October fifteenth."

"Is that today?"

My nod satisfied him. The pressure of his fingers on mine

sent me reeling. His touch, firm and gentle at the same time, reassured me.

"I c-can come… c-come home n-now?"

Tears fell to hear him say the word *home.* I had begun to wonder if some of these men might rather stay here in relative safety, with no challenges from the outside world.

Gabe dried one of my tears with his finger and pulled me close, the puzzle forgotten. Every other consideration vanished for me, too. In spite of the inescapable hospital odors, Gabe's scent inundated me. His shoulders and arms had shrunken, true. He'd been hurt, yes, but he was still Gabe.

He *knew* me—he could walk and talk. He could think… and feel. This frightful old war had not stolen Gabriel Andretti from me.

The next day, the nurse said yesterday went so well that we could go outside. On a bench in a courtyard behind the massive hospital building, I pulled something from my purse, and Gabe held it in his hands.

"Lavender? You brought me lavender!"

"Thought you might like a little of this year's crop. Last year, your mother took over the distilling, but even a small bottle takes so much of the harvest. I wonder if we might need to plant another field?"

His eyes sparkled. "Oh, I need to get h-home. The d-doc…"

"What does he say?"

"D-don't get… don't h-hurry."

"Whenever they let you go, the land will be there waiting for you. And I've brought pictures, too. Here… see Luke and Bella with Sam?"

"L-Luke." Gabe shook his head. "And w-we have…"

"Gabby." I showed him another photograph. "He weighs almost as much as Luke—he's going to be one big man."

"T-taller than…"

"Me for sure, and maybe you, too."

"And B-bella… she looks s-so much l-like you."

"But she learns her lessons like you. Always out in front of her class."

Gabe's sigh ran deep. We went inside to the craft room, and he glanced at a puzzle. "They say doing these'll help my fingers work better. Whatever it t-takes, I say, to g-get home."

Walking back to Bea's, I breathed deep of this Texas air, not as dry as Arizona's. Something about it—perhaps the essence of sage—took me back to our house during the black blizzards.

Bea said she and Joe married after the rest of us moved on and soon had their own brood to care for. Joe had trouble finding work at first, so they eventually moved to the city, where new buildings were going up all the time. Things had gone well for them, thanks to his carpentry skills. Always apologetic about not writing, Bea expressed regret that I was only now getting to know her children. Cyril, with a part-time job and school, I rarely saw, but the other three—fourteen, twelve, and nine—kept me busy in the evenings.

"I never forgot you, and somewhere along the way, Suzie wrote to me. Have you kept in touch with any of the others?"

"I haven't. Gabe will have enough of a surprise to hear me talk about you and Suzie."

"When this is all over, we've got to keep in touch, all right? And before you leave, I hope to meet Gabe."

"I'll ask the nurse about extra visitors. Just two days left."

"Tomorrow afternoon Joe needs me at his office, so it'll have to be Friday. Can't believe this time has gone so fast." Bea knitted socks for the troops, and kept her needles clicking this whole time.

I asked her for a lesson, and after half an hour, she pronounced me a fast learner. "The Red Cross will supply your yarn if you're knitting socks, sweaters, or scarves. It's a good pastime, too—keeps me from worrying about Cyril."

The nurse said my visits were making a big difference for Gabe and gave permission for us to leave the grounds for a walk to Bea's place the next day. "But be back by three, okay?"

Gabe seemed brighter. His gait had slowed from before the war, but his leg dragged less than the day before—or was that my imagination?

It didn't matter—he was so excited to get out into the world. Every rabbit we saw munching in people's gardens astounded him, each street sign brought something new to mind. He greeted every passerby we met—I had to agree with his nurse, I was *good medicine* for him.

At Bea's, we surveyed her garden, ate sandwiches, and drank lemonade. The time was passing so quickly—it had taken nearly twenty minutes to get there.

Then Gabe's eyes changed. I knew that look. He stood and pulled me up. "Where do you sleep?"

"Over there, in a sun porch."

"Show me." His whisper grazed my cheek, and I melted. Indeed, this was the old Gabe, through-and-through. But what if he… could he hurt himself?

He read my concern just like always. "Don't worry. I'm f-fine." He unbuttoned his shirt.

His scars startled me. So many of them, some still red and sore-looking, yet none bandaged. I smoothed the largest with my fingers.

"I'm so sorry for what you went through over there…"

He tossed his head, and I visualized those dark curls grown out a bit more. "Everybody d-did. It's j-just the war, th-that's all."

"Just a minute." I hurried to my purse and opened a small vial. Ever so gently, I rubbed lavender oil into his scars until he replaced the lid and pulled me down, pulled me so close I could scarcely breathe.

Chapter Ten

Christmas 1944, with Gabe home at last. He insisted on cutting down a tree, hauling it in with Bella and Luca, and starting the fire in the woodstove by himself. This year we have gone all out, decking the mantle with cedar and lighting candles in every window.

Every night since we came home—he used his debate skills to convince the doctors he'd healed enough to accompany me when I left San Antonio—he has sat with Bella, Luca, and Gabby in his arms. They all fit, and I crowded in to listen to the news reports, which seem not to bother Gabe.

Maybe it's because everyone is so certain the fighting in Europe will soon end. As for the Pacific Front, he reads every newspaper article he can find.

"Those boys, n-now. Th-they really have it tough. I hear the Japs are ten times w-worse than the G-germans."

After the news, we tuck everyone in and he tells a story about bees discovering the deep woods of…this time it's Mississippi and Alabama. He hints about an Indian boy in Oklahoma who will soon enjoy the bees' honey and names the boy after one of his buddies from the war.

Later, we feed the fire and embrace the evening quiet. Tonight, though, we tune in to President Roosevelt's Christmas address to the nation.

> *It is not easy to say "Merry Christmas" to you, my fellow Americans, in this time of destructive war. Nor can I say "Merry Christmas" lightly tonight to our armed forces at their battle*

stations all over the world—or to our allies who fight by their side.

Here, at home, we will celebrate this Christmas Day in our traditional American way—because of its deep spiritual meaning to us; because the teachings of Christ are fundamental in our lives; and because we want our youngest generation to grow up knowing the significance of this tradition and the story of the coming of the immortal Prince of Peace and Good Will. But, in perhaps every home in the United States, sad and anxious thoughts will be continually with the millions of our loved ones who are suffering hardships and misery, and who are risking their very lives to preserve for us and for all mankind the fruits of His teachings and the foundations of civilization itself.

The Christmas spirit lives tonight in the bitter cold of the front lines in Europe and in the heat of the jungles and swamps of Burma and the Pacific islands. Even the roar of our bombers and fighters in the air and the guns of our ships at sea will not drown out the messages of Christmas which come to the hearts of our fighting men. The thoughts of these men tonight will turn to us here at home around our Christmas trees, surrounded by our children and grandchildren and their Christmas stockings and gifts—just as our own thoughts go out to them, tonight and every night, in their distant places.

We all know how anxious they are to be home with us, and they know how anxious we are to have them—and how determined every one of us is to make their day of home-coming as early as possible. And—above all—they know the determination of all right-thinking people and Nations, that Christmases such as those that we have known in these years of world tragedy shall not come again to beset the souls of the children of God.

This generation has passed through many recent years of deep darkness, watching the spread of the poison of Hitlerism and Fascism in Europe—the growth of imperialism and militarism in Japan—and the final clash of war all over the world.

Then came the dark days of the fall of France, and the ruthless bombing of England, and the desperate battle of the Atlantic, and of Pearl Harbor and Corregidor and Singapore.

Since then the prayers of good men and women and children the world over have been answered. The tide of battle has turned, slowly but inexorably, against those who sought to destroy civilization.

On this Christmas day, we cannot yet say when our victory will come. Our enemies still fight fanatically. They still have reserves of men and military power. But, they themselves know that they and their evil works are doomed. We may hasten the day of their doom if we here at home continue to do our full share.

And we pray that that day may come soon. We pray that until then, God will protect our gallant men and women in the uniforms of the United Nations—that He will receive into His infinite grace those who make their supreme sacrifice in the cause of righteousness, in the cause of love of Him and His teachings.

We pray that with victory will come a new day of peace on earth in which all the Nations of the earth will join together for all time. That is the spirit of Christmas, the holy day. May that spirit live and grow throughout the world in all the years to come.

Gabe falls silent now, and really, what is there to say? He goes out for a walk alone, and from the darkened house, I watch him pass through our lavender field, up and down the rows. How can he not be thinking of his unit still engaged in the war?

Even though we're married, there are some places I cannot go with him, some memories too divorced from our simple life here. And that's as it should be. We still have plenty to share.

On some nights, we fall asleep on the couch. This new freedom comes as a gift, since Antonio married Bernardo as soon as he finished their house in late November. When she took me for a tour, I asked how she could leave her lovely home—our house now—after all these years.

Her answer? "It's not-a the house. It's the man."

Ah… who would have guessed Antonia would remarry and live less than a mile across the canyon? She comes over every day and finally has stopped telling Gabe to quit working so hard.

She still works with the distiller, since Gabe doesn't trust his hands with the delicate glass tubes yet. And the bees—they have become her sole domain.

Gabe and Bernardo hit it off right away. Gabe allows that some jobs he used to handle alone now require help, and the two of them compare notes on beekeeping.

Every morning, Gabe and Luca walk Bella to school and fetch her in the afternoons. Already, his limp has lessened, and as one of his doctors predicted, his stuttering has decreased.

"Third time's a charm!" Antonia pronounces this blessing when we gather for dinner on Christmas Day. "Three years we waited for you to come home."

"Charm! Time!" Luca echoes. He turns to Bella and burbles on about Daddy being here at last.

Today Bernardo's family is joining us, and his daughter Lolita brings as much food as Antonia and I make. A good mix, *las pambazas, los tamales,* and *los churros.*

Who says one cannot wrap a tender Italian meatball in a scrumptious homemade tortilla? And I wonder… *Could I make los tamales with a lavender lemon chicken filling?* Now that the war truly is close-to-over, it's time to celebrate our cultures and blend our wisdom.

After everyone has feasted and Bernardo sees his family home, Gabe naps with all three children. I putter in the kitchen, thinking of Mama. Suzie, who comes one day a week to help with the children, reminds me that when Mama passed, everything happened so quickly. No one had time to say good-bye.

Still, I wish I could have seen her just once more—near the end of her life, maybe something would have shifted. Going to the funeral seemed other-worldly, as if the pastor were describing someone I had never met. He noted Mama's faithfulness, and how involved she became during the previous year filling boxes for European refugees.

At that point I glanced over at Suzie, who gave a slight smirk. How ironic, she told me later, that Antonia's project spread to the Methodist ladies, who have been happily sending refugee packages, too.

Later, Gabe hoists Gabby, and we walk through the lavender field together. Luca and Bella never seem to tire of this evening stroll. Not once has Gabe mentioned his time away since he came home in October, but now he does.

"Today reminded me of the Army." He kicks at a rock, sending it bouncing for Luca to find. "Different kinds of people together for a mission."

"Except we didn't have to sacrifice the way you did."

"True."

"And our mission was to devour a lot of food?"

"Something like that."

"Lossa food!" Luca races up and slams into Gabe's leg, so Gabe hands me our sleepy Gabby and throws Luca in the air. He responds with wild giggles, and Bella cries, "Me too, Daddy! Me too!"

Despite his injuries, Gabe has no trouble complying with his daughter's wishes. We have so very much to give thanks for.

Postlude

Summer, 1947

Gabe has Luca and Bella out harvesting lavender. When he says, "Not this year, Gabby, maybe next summer. You stay here and help Mommy with the twins," Gabby puts up a fuss worthy of Grandma Antonia.

She's out there working, too, with Bernardo and one of his grandsons. I've opened every window in the house to let in the heavenly fragrance, but it's a bit too soon after the twins' birth for me to bend down to cut stems.

Our family is complete now, Gabe likes to say, since Dominic and Isadora have joined us. I agree, but *we'll see* makes a handy philosophy in matters like this.

We have given Antonia her wish… a grandson named Dominic. I forget exactly when she said, "If you have another boy, call him Dominic. Isn't that a beautiful name? And it means, *Lordly*. Don't you think he would have to be to survive life with his wild older brothers?"

Yes, our family does seem complete with two girls and three boys, but if we're blessed with a sixth child, that will be all right, too. When the doctor announced that he heard two heartbeats, Bernardo fashioned two matching cribs, and we've moved them into the living room, with another two upstairs.

Gabe and I take turns in the night when the twins can't get to sleep. Exhausted, we lie on the floor between the two, get a good grip on each crib and swing them both back and forth. Usually this technique works.

Dominic's going to be musical, prophesies Antonia, and Isadora will get involved in politics one day. When we ask about her reasoning she claims, "A feeling I have. Just a feeling."

Perhaps this has to do with rumors of General Dwight Eisenhower running for President in the next election year. In retrospect, Antonia has laid aside her judgment of the errors our commanders made during the war and sees him as a hero who guided us to victory.

How does she view President Truman? Roosevelt was no easy act to follow, she says.

Her feelings make quite a study. Like believing the rosary-over-the-clothesline would help protect Gabe during the war, teaming in childhood with Concetta Spagnoletti as her best friend forever, realizing at age fourteen that Luca would be her husband, and falling for Bernardo the first time she saw him working at the church.

For Antonia, feeling a certain way and knowing it to be true amount to the same thing. Makes life simpler.

Gabe's nightly children's stories still continue. Sometime last summer, the bees that crossed the Atlantic and started their inland journey at the Jamestown Colony finally reached Arizona's forests.

"Like the Tonto?" Bella, with her growing sense of geography, requires specifics.

"Yes, they flew right into the Tonto Basin."

By Thanksgiving, those bees had viewed the beautiful Pacific Ocean from forested areas above the Coast. Then they wended northward to Washington State. To help everyone visualize the movement, Gabe has created a wooden puzzle, a map of the United States.

Up in the corner, he carved a skep—a dome-shaped basket—to show how the bees crossed the ocean in the first settlers' ships. This puzzle keeps little hands busy during the day, too.

When Gabby sees a bee in the lavender or in our garden, he

gets so excited. Of course, Daddy has explained that even though bees are our friends and give us such delectable honey, they do not like to be caught. It took a few tries for Gabby to realize that holding a bee isn't in the plan, and I'm sure he'll soon be teaching this truth to his little brother and sister.

"Doesn't he ever stop talking?" Hearing Gabe ask this makes me smile—he missed this season of Luca's childhood. Gabby and Luca, like their daddy, will most likely be debaters one day—it's a mark of the Andretti family.

Whatever is to come, the war has ended, providing constant cause for rejoicing. Antonia's packages still find their way to the refugees in Europe as the rebuilding continues there. And here, there's a sense of hope as new businesses begin. Returned soldiers build houses and buy automobiles, school districts have to build more classrooms, and all is bustling.

Laughter comes easier these days. *Might as well be cheerful*—I think this often. *Why not fill our rambling home with giggles and chuckles, love and good feelings? We've had our share of worries and fear.*

Why not focus on life's sweet side? Why not smile our way through the years and keep the windows open to the buzzing of the bees and the lavender's heady fragrance?

Recipes

Lavender Honey Ice Cream

Ingredients
    1.5 cups cream
    1.5 cups milk
    1/2 cup lavender honey
    1 tsp royal velvet lavender buds

Steep lavender buds in warmed milk for 10 minutes, add honey and stir until liquid.
Strain off buds.
Add the cooled lavender honey milk and the cream to your ice cream maker and churn as directed!

Pine Creek Lavender Farm Sugar

Ingredients
    1 cup regular granulated white sugar
    1 tbsp Royal Velvet Dried Lavender

In a high-speed blender, add sugar and top with dried lavender. Blend at medium high speed for about 30 seconds or until lavender is completely pulverized into sugar.

The sugar will be broken down into an almost powdered sugar consistency. Do not double or over blend the sugar. It will get overheated and begin to melt.

Store as you would any sugar.

Lasts almost indefinitely, so make up a big batch for baking too!

Apple Jelly with Lemon & Lavender

Ingredients
4 lbs apples to yield 4 cups apple juice (I used Ida Reds)
1 small lemon, preferably organic
3 tbsp lemon juice (fresh or bottled)
1 cup filtered water
1 tsp dried culinary lavender
pinch salt
2 1/2 cups raw sugar (organic turbinado)

Method
Scrub the apples, quarter, cut off stem and blossom ends, then place in a stockpot with cool filtered water just to cover. Bring to a simmer over medium-high heat; lower heat and simmer until apples are soft, about 30 minutes.

Strain apples through a jelly bag or several layers of dampened cheesecloth to collect juice. This is best done *overnight* so that any sediment in the juices will be able to fall to the bottom.

Reserve the pulp for butter, sauce, or leather.

The next day, prepare canner, jars, and lids.

Scrub the lemon well and slice into very thin rounds. Pick out any seeds that did not fall out on their own, and spread slices in a single layer in a large preserving pot or Dutch oven.

Add 1 cup filtered water and poach lemon slices over medium heat until lemon rinds are transparent (timing depends on how thin you can make your slices; mine took about 15 minutes, but some slices remained stubbornly opaque). Add additional water if lemon slices begin to stick and caramelize.

Add 4 cups of apple juice to the pot, along with lemon juice, lavender, sugar, and salt. Bring to a boil over high heat, stirring just until the sugar is dissolved.

Continue to boil hard, skimming foam occasionally, until jelly reaches the set point: 220 degrees F on an instant thermometer, or a small dollop on a frozen plate forms wrinkles after freezing for 1 to 2 minutes.

Boil hard at the set point for 1 minute, then turn off heat.

Ladle hot jelly into hot jars; fill to 1/4-inch headspace. Wipe rims, affix lids and process in a boiling water bath for 10 minutes.

Yields about 4 cups.

Herbs de Provence

Ingredients
    1/4 cup dried thyme
    3 tbsp dried marjoram
    3 tbsp dried summer savory, optional
    1 tbsp dried tarragon
    1 tbsp dried basil
    1 tsp dried chervil, optional
    1 tsp dried mint
    1 tsp dried lavender, optional

Italian Lemon Cake with Lavender Glaze

This is an old Italian recipe that was made fashionable by its unique use of just a pan, a bowl, and a tablespoon as the only utensils needed to make. But don't let its simplicity fool you—this cake is as good as any lemon cake you have ever eaten. Enjoy!

Ingredients by level Tablespoons
    12 tbsp all-purpose flour
    1 tsp baking powder
    10 tbsp Pine Creek Lavender Sugar
    2 eggs (large)
    zest of 2 lemons
    3 tbsp lemon juice
    10 tbsp quality oil such as avocado or grapeseed
    10 tbsp milk or nondairy milk

5 easy steps to make your new fav cake!
Beat egg and sugar until light and very fluffy (4+ minutes)
Mix in zest, lemon juice, milk and oil
Add flour and baking powder; beat until smooth
Pour into prepared cake or Bundt pan; Bake 350 for 40 min. (use a 7 or 8 inch pan or double the recipe for larger)

Glaze: Mix 3–4 tbsp lavender sugar with 2–3 tbsp lemon juice plus 1 tbsp zest. Pour over cake while still warm.

Italian Pepper Short Ribs Peposo

Peposo—a Tuscan Red Wine Stew is a traditional Tuscan Beef Stew originating from Florence. It truly is the simplest stew you'll ever make yet it has so much flavor. Made with garlic, lots of black pepper, and a whole bottle of red wine it is super delicious and perfect served with creamy polenta.

Ingredients
   2 lbs beef chuck or shank or stewing beef (1 kg) cut into 1 inch cubes
   1 bottle red wine Chianti or Sangiovese if possible
   6 whole garlic cloves peeled
   2 tbsp freshly ground black pepper
   1 tsp sea salt flakes or kosher salt
   1 tbsp olive oil

Prep Time5 minutes
Cook Time3 hours
Total Time3 hours 5 minutes
Servings4–6 servings

Heat the olive oil in a large pot, brown the beef on all sides for a minute or two (you might need to do this in batches so there is enough room).
Add the beef and juices back to the pot (if browning in batches)

and add the red wine, garlic, salt and pepper.

Cover the pot with a lid and simmer on a medium-low heat for 1.5 hours, uncover the pot and continue to simmer the stew for another 1.5 hours until the liquid has reduced slightly.

Top tip: once the stew is uncovered check it every so often and give it a stir to make sure it doesn't stick or the meat at the top dries out.

The beef should be tender but not completely falling apart. Serve with creamy polenta and crusty bread.

Rick's Pine Creek Farm Lavender Peposo

Rick is Italian through and through. Born in Pittsburgh, Pennsylvania, Rick grew up in an all Italian family and neighborhood. He inherited his amazing culinary skills from both his Mom and Dad, who were cooks and bakers extraordinaire.

This is Rick and sons', Andy, Aj, and Luke's, hands down favorite beef dish from the Farm—and always on the Christmas table!

Don't be concerned or be tempted to reduce all the pepper; it mellows to a rich deep flavor as it becomes infused in the wine!

Ingredients
   3 tbsp Olive Oil
   6 bone-in beef short ribs (about 8 to 10 ounces each)
   1 tbsp Pine Creek Farm Lavender Himalayan Salt to coat the short ribs
   8 cloves garlic, peeled and crushed
   1 tbsp tomato paste
   2 tbsp Pine Creek Farm Lavender Lemon Pepper, freshly crushed or ground.
   1 additional tbsp freshly ground Pine Creek Farm Lavender Lemon Pepper.
   3–4 small sage leaves
   3–4 small sprigs dried lavender leaves or rosemary can be used too
   2 cups red wine, preferably Chianti

2 bay leaves
Pine Creek Lavender Himalayan salt to taste, to adjust sauce

Heat the olive oil in a large, heavy bottom Dutch oven, brown the short ribs on all sides for a minute or two, grinding the Lavender Salt over as you brown the meat (you might need to do this in batches so there is enough room).

Next, Add all the short ribs, the tomato paste, Pine Creek Lavender Lemon Pepper, spices, garlic and wine to the pot you browned the meat in.

Cover and simmer on a medium-low heat for about 1.5 hours, uncover and grind the remaining tablespoon of Pine Creek Lavender Lemon Pepper and Lavender Salt to adjust the taste. Recover and continue to simmer, for another 1.5–2 hours, turning occasionally until the wine has been absorbed and the sauce has reduced.

The short ribs should be fork tender but not completely falling apart.

At the farm, we serve the Peposo over creamy polenta and always have some crusty, warm Italian bread to soak up any of the incredible sauce.

Serves 6

Manga!

Lavender Blackberry Jam

Ingredients
For 6-7 half pint jars of jam, you will need:
    5 cups crushed blackberries
    1 package powdered pectin
    5-6 cups Pine Creek Lavender Sugar (sugar will vary by ripeness of berries)
    ¼ cup lemon juice (optional)
    (Terry's Note: Many fruits contain natural pectin and their jams can be made without pectin and/or by using low or no sugar pectin)

Sort and wash fully ripe blackberries; remove any stems or green berries.

Crush berries. (Option: If you want a seedless jam, put part or all of them through a sieve or food mill.)

Measure 5 cups crushed berries into a non-reactive kettle. Add pectin and stir well.

Place on high heat and, stirring constantly, bring quickly to a full boil

Add Lavender sugar, continue stirring. Return to a full rolling boil that cannot be stirred down.

Boil hard for 1 minute, stirring constantly. Remove from heat; skim.

Fill hot jam immediately into hot, sterile jars, leaving ¼ inch headspace.

Wipe rims of jars. Apply lids and rings and adjust.
Process in a Boiling Water Canner. (see below)
Remove from canner. Cool. Check seals. Label date and Store.

Note: when canning at high altitudes when processing Hot Pack using pint or half-pint jars:
0–1,000 ft—5minutes
1,000–6,000 ft—10 minutes
Above 6,000 ft—15 minutes

Mexican Pambazos (with a lavender twist)

Ingredients
    4 buns bolillo or telera bread sliced lengthwise
For the sauce
    6 dry guajillo chiles, deveined
    1 cup hot water
    1 minced clove garlic
    1/2 tsp dry oregano
    Salt to taste (1/2 tsp kosher salt)
    Pre-cook potatoes
    12 oz diced
    Enough water to cover and cook the potatoes
    Salt the water generously
    For the chorizo filling
    1 lb pork or beef chorizo
    1 garlic clove, minced
    1/2 small yellow onion, diced
    Salt to taste
    Olive oil
    Assemble the sandwiches using additional ingredients
    Shredded lettuce
    Mexican style cream
    Queso fresco, crumbled
    Salsa
    Avocado

Lavender bud sprinkles

Directions
Peel and dice potatoes
Cook in salted boiling water over medium heat (about 6-7 minutes. Remove from heat, drain and run through cold water. Drain the water once again and set aside for later use.

Devein and toast the guajillos over low heat. Turn continuously to prevent them from burning. Once fragrant and toasted on both sides, remove from the heat and rinse them. Place in a container and pour in hot water to rehydrate and soften them, (about 5 minutes).

Pine Canyon Lavender Spa Wellness Soak

Ingredients
    2 cups Epsom salt
    1 cup Baking soda
    1 tbsp Fresh Lavender (optional)
    10 to 12 drops of lavender essential oil
    Pink Himalayan Salt Granules

Directions
Mix the soda and salts in a large bowl. Add the Pine Creek Canyon Lavender Essential Oils, a few drops at a time, mixing thoroughly as you incorporate the oils.

Add fresh lavender at the end and mix again. Let sit out, mixing occasionally for another 30 minutes.

Store in sealed containers. Add 1/2 to 2 cups to your bath. Enjoy!

Lavender Lemon Pepper Green Chile Pulled Chicken Tamale Filling

Ingredients
  1–2 Tbsp avocado or olive oil
  1/2 cup white or yellow onion, diced (optional)
  2 cloves garlic, minced
  Pine Lavender Himalayan Salt + other optional cumin, etc.
  1 cup diced hatch chiles, or other fav varieties like Jalapenos
or Poblanos
  2–2 ½ cups shredded chicken

Directions
Warm oil and saute onion, garlic and Lavender Lemon Pepper until well done.
  Add shredded chicken, heat thru adjusting salt and spices to taste.
  Add chilies and combine. Cool to handle the mixture.

You're Ready to Get Makin Tamales Now!
Spoon masa on soaked (I hour in warm water) husks; add pulled chicken filling; fold and tie tamales.
  After you have assembled the tamales, use a tamale steamer or fashion your own and steam cook them for approximately 1 hour or until the masa pulls away clean from the corn husk.
  Top with your favorite salsa, cilantro, sour cream or plain and enjoy!

Pine Creek Lavender Farm Sugar:

Ingredients
    one cup regular granulated white sugar
    1 tbsp Royal Velvet Dried Lavender

Directions
In a high-speed blender like a Vitamix, put one cup regular granulated white sugar. Top with 1 tbsp Royal Velvet Dried Lavender. Blend at medium high speed for about 30 seconds or until lavender is completely pulverized into sugar.

The sugar will be broken down into an almost powdered sugar consistency.

Do not double or over-blend the sugar. It will get overheated and begin to melt.

Store as you would any sugar. Lasts almost indefinitely, so make up a big batch for baking too!

Acknowledgements

Thanks to Terry Vesci and The Pine Creek Canyon Lavender Farm for her encouragement and help with lavender research. Visit Terry online at:

www.pinelavenderfarm.com

Also, I'm very grateful to Cathy Fiorello for lending her expertise during this writing project. Visit Cathy online at:

www.cathyfiorello.com

About the Author

Words have always been comfort food for Gail Kittleson. After instructing expository writing and English as a Second Language, she began writing seriously. Intrigued by the World War II era, Gail creates historical fiction from her northern Iowa home and also facilitates writing workshops/retreats.

She and her husband, a retired Army chaplain, enjoy grandchildren and in winter, Arizona's Mogollon Rim Country. You can count on Gail's protagonists to ask honest questions, act with integrity, grow in faith, and face hardships with spunk.

Visit Gail online at:

www.GailKittleson.com

Also by Gail Kittleson

Women of the Heartland Series

In Times Like These
With Each New Dawn
A Purpose True
All for the Cause
Until Then
&
Kiss Me Once Again
a Women of the Heartland story

and

The Winds of Change
A Mystery on Church Street
Land That I Love
Secondhand Sunsets

Also available from

WordCrafts Press

The Pruning
by Jan Cline

Plague
by Marian Rizzo

Oh to Grace!
by Abby Rosser

The Restless Earth
by Alan Cockrell

The Gift
by Cheri Dargan

www.WordCrafts.net